CW01627207

THE SISTER-IN-LAW

LOUISE KERR

Copyright © 2025 Black Swan Digital

The right of Black Swan Digital to be identified as the Author of the Work

has been asserted by her in accordance Copyright, Designs and Patents Act 1988.

First published in 2025

Concept created by Black Swan Digital. Developed by Flo Hurt.

Apart from any use permitted under UK copyright law, this publication may only be reproduced, stored, or transmitted, in any form, or by any means, with prior permission in writing of the author or, in the case of reprographic production, in accordance with the terms of licences issued by the Copyright Licensing Agency.

All characters in this publication are fictitious and any resemblance to real persons, living or dead, is purely coincidental.

PROLOGUE

I don't remember waking, only the quiet after the storm broke. It was the kind of quiet that isn't quiet at all. Rain rattling the gutters, the wind worrying the eaves, a draught running its cold fingers along the skirting boards. The house felt hollowed out.

I lay there and held my breath, listening for the thing that didn't fit.

There. A sound. Not loud. Not clear. It was a *click* noise that could've been anything, but became an intruder opening and closing a door to my sleepy mind.

I told myself it was nothing. Old houses breathe. They expand, contract. Pipes cough. Timber settles. *It's just the house settling*. How many times had I heard that phrase?

The bedside clock blinked 02:13, then suddenly went black. Power cut? The wind moaned down the chimney and a branch scraped against the window. The darkness became eerily thick. I reached out for my phone.

Dead. Of course. No light, no signal.

I got up.

On the landing, the air smelled of damp and something sweeter underneath. Lavender? Fabric softener? I tried to make it something civilised and acceptable so that paranoia wouldn't get the better of me. The carpet was cool beneath my feet. My fingers found the banister, and I stood still until my eyes adjusted to the darkness. Shapes bled through the black. Picture frames. A chair. The lean, tall rectangle of a door that should have been shut.

"Nursery," I whispered.

I hadn't said that word out loud in months. It pulsed with a hint of danger and regret. I said it now as if to punish myself in a sick way.

The door was ajar just enough to show a slice of pale wall, a shadow where a curtain fell, the lighter strip of carpet that the hinge didn't quite cover. I was sure I'd closed it earlier. I was *certain.*

"Hello?" My voice sounded far too small and helpless.

I crossed the landing. Each step was impossibly loud. I got the warped sense the house was listening.

My hand hesitated at the edge of the door, hovered there. It wasn't fear, I told myself. It was caution. Caution is sensible. Caution is what keeps you alive when the familiar begins to feel wrong. I was protecting myself. Not just physically, but my mind too.

The door moved with a soft complaint, wood on wood as if it didn't want me to come in, and then the room opened.

The cot beneath the window was made up neatly, the sheet tucked tight, the blanket smoothed with a sure hand. It was ready. A mobile hung from the ceiling: moons and stars that should have spun but didn't, as if the air here obeyed a different set of rules.

No dust. No disorder. Everything too clean, too arranged.

I stepped inside. The floor was colder here, as if the heat of the house didn't want to cross the threshold. I didn't switch on a light. But even in the dark, the outlines were clear enough: a life waiting to be lived. Someone had chosen carefully. Someone had wanted the room to be gentle.

I stood at the cot and stared down at the emptiness where a tiny body might go. My hands rose without being told to. They hovered for a heartbeat above the rail, then they closed around it.

Warm.

Not the ghost of warmth that wood holds after a day of sun. Not the illusion of warmth that numb fingers invent. Warm, as though a hand had been there a moment ago, the skin-to-skin of presence still pressed into the grain.

I snatched my hands back.

"Is someone here?"

The mobile answered with a faint squeak. The curtains breathed again. The house said nothing, though it felt, somehow, like it had a lot to say.

I told myself to think. To list the facts. Power cut. Wind. An open door. A room dressed for a child that doesn't exist. Warmth where there should be none. There are explanations for everything. There always are.

A floorboard behind me groaned.

I turned so fast the room jerked. The doorway was an empty black. The landing beyond was the same. No shape. No movement. But the feeling of being watched came all the same, prickling the back of my neck with a tingle of fight-or-flight danger.

"Who's there?" I demanded, trying to sound brave... and probably failing.

Silence.

Then, so soft I might have imagined it, a whisper. It sounded as if could have come from the landing or the room behind me. Or, terrifyingly, the inside of my own skull.

"Mine," it breathed, inhuman.

I didn't move at first. I tried to hear it again, praying I was going insane and hadn't really heard it, praying it was real at the same time. I tried to tame the sound, to turn it into a radiator complaining, a gutter gasping, the wind forcing its way into the bones of the house.

I became aware of my heart. It was not beating in my chest. It was beating everywhere: wrists, throat, the tips of my fingers. A pulse in the soles of my feet. I took a step back. The cot's shadow slid across the floor like a hand that wanted to choke me.

I stepped into the hall and the atmosphere of the house changed. *Go back to bed. You're being silly.* The lavender vanished, as if somebody thought the scent was too sweet for the likes of me.

"Hello?" I said again, louder, with more stubborn desire to sound tough. I wasn't being hunted by a monster. I *was* the monster.

No answer.

I moved from door to door like a sleepwalker on a tour of her own life, opening, peering, closing. I found no one.

Back on the landing, the nursery door had drifted further open, as though the house were breathing it wider with each inhale. I didn't want to go back inside. I didn't want to look again at the cot, at the chair, at the everyday mercy of the rabbit picture on the wall.

"Mine," someone, some*thing* whispered. The word felt closer this time, more certain, like a hidden predator was getting tired of me not getting the point; it was preparing to pounce.

This was getting absurd. I slammed the door hard, heard the *click*. It should've been reassuring, but I couldn't help but think of the *click* I'd heard earlier.

I stood there, palm flat against the paint, counting. Three, for the Father. Three, for the Son. Three, for the Holy Ghost. Old superstitions are the scaffolding we cling to when the walls rearrange themselves.

When I turned to go back to bed, the stairs fell away into a darkness that looked more threatening than before. The banister curved down like a beckoning finger. I felt suddenly that if I went down, something would be waiting at the bottom.

I did not go down.

I went into the bedroom and sat on the edge of the bed. The power made a half-hearted attempt at life. The bedside clock blinked 02:17, then nothing. How had such little time passed? The house seemed to reconsider and settle on the idea that night would be longer than usual.

My breath made a cold patch in the air that dissolved before I could see it properly. I thought of calling someone, then remembered my dead mobile, the power cut that made the landline useless. I thought of waking him, *no, not him, there is no him here, not tonight, not now,* and found I couldn't even think his name, as if the dark had stolen not just light but language.

The house stopped groaning. The ordinary noises of night crept back in. I lay down, eyes on the door, waiting for a monster that didn't come.

I didn't sleep.

Near dawn the power returned with a small, apologetic hum. The clock stuttered into 06:01. The heating pipes woke and cleared their throats. Downstairs the fridge began to purr. The house pretended it had been ordinary all along. I knew the feeling. We all do, don't we?

When I finally accepted sleep wouldn't be coming that night, or rather the morning, I rose and went to the landing.

The nursery door stood open again. A gasp escaped me. It sounded melodramatic even to my own ears. But screw it. If I couldn't be melodramatic now, when could I?

I could have told myself I hadn't closed it properly. I could have told myself that draughts and gravity and the shifting of wood were explanations enough. I could have told myself anything I liked. But I knew every so-called explanation would've been a lie.

I didn't go in. Not then. I stood there with the morning growing around me and thought of some hidden thing, inhuman or worse, a man in a balaclava with sick desires pumping hotly through his veins, slipping from his hiding place and opening the door I had closed. Opening a piece of myself I wanted to bury.

"Mine," it had said.

A door is only a door, I thought. A room is only a room. My too-tired mind spit out these nothing phrases as if to offer comfort.

It failed.

The house had already chosen another story. And I had already, whether I wanted to or not, begun to believe it.

1

October 19th

The Keaton house had the kind of quiet that money buys. Not silence, but a curated hush, where even the tick of the longcase clock in the hall seemed like a quiet cheerleader, congratulating them on their well-to-do lives. Lucy stood on the black-and-white tiles in the entranceway and watched her reflection bend on their gloss: a woman with careful lipstick, a dress that didn't quite feel like hers, a coat chosen because the shop assistant had said "classic" and she'd wanted that word to be true. Lucy wanted so many things to be true. Even her reflection was a twisted wish. She couldn't see herself in such high-definition detail. Self-consciousness was getting the better of her.

She wanted tonight to go well. She wanted to be the daughter-in-law Susan and Henry deserved.

Ed shook off his coat and ran a hand through his hair. "Mother?" he called out.

Susan's reply carried down the corridor. "In the dining room, darling."

The dining room was all polish, like everything Keaton-related. Lucy warned herself not to get bitter. This was *her* world now too.

Heavy curtains framed a garden with leaves arranged on the grass as if someone had sprinkled them with deliberation. On the long table, silver gleamed in controlled ranks, the cutlery aligned as though the meal were a military operation. The air smelled of roast beef and bay leaves and something sweet waiting its turn.

Susan stood at the head of the table, a pearl at her throat, her pale hair turned neatly at the ends, a woman who had never once left the house with a ladder in her tights or popped to the shop in a pair of slippers.

Henry was at her shoulder, half eclipsed by the high back of one of the chairs, his wine already poured, his smile already faint and polite. He looked like her pet or employee.

Bad Lucy. He's your father-in-law. Have some respect.

"Lucy." Susan moved forward to kiss the air near Lucy's cheek, as if real contact was far too much in*deed*. "You look... nice." She let her eyes skim the dress as if contemplating setting it on fire. Maybe even with Lucy still wearing it. "Is that new?"

"It is," Lucy said. "Thank you."

"It suits you," Susan added, with the air of repeating a rote phrase that must be said for the sake of decorum. "Edward, hang your wife's coat properly, please. The hooks in the hall, not on the banister. This isn't a halfway house."

Ed laughed and did as he was told. He always did as he was told in this house; Lucy could feel it, a soft choreography older than she was, more important than she was, even. He came back to her side and squeezed her hand. It was a small, private reassurance.

It's like he doesn't want them to see, she thought cynically. *He's afraid they'll think I'm weak.*

This was classic Lucy. Projecting. Big time.

"Father," Ed said, "you've been raiding the cellar."

Father. Not *Dad*, but *Father*, a not-so-subtle reminder that they were from a different world than her.

Henry lifted his glass in a quiet salute. "Sundays demand it."

Ed chuckled and winked. "Every day demands it, let's be honest."

Henry looked into his glass for a few moments and took a sip with the air of a man used to being bullied.

Lucy smiled. "The food smells wonderful, Susan."

"Mrs Keaton," Susan snapped like a reflex.

For long moments, the atmosphere was tense. Lucy waited for Henry to ride to her rescue, but he didn't.

Susan finally relented with a gracious tilt of her head. "As you're family now, Susan will do." She returned to the table, adjusted a napkin without looking at it, and said, "Shall we? The beef will be just right."

As they took their places, that phrase bounced around Lucy's mind. *Susan will do.* She was related to them now. Part of the family. But, of course, her first name was some Holy Grail she had to beg and scrape to be able to use. It was gross.

Lucy had rehearsed not making a fuss about where to sit, only to find her chair was already marked out by a small card, handwritten in Susan's neat script. "How lovely," she said, because it was obviously what the matriarch slash queen slash empress was expecting.

"Form," Susan said. "It matters more than people think." She set the tone with a smile that could have been read as kind by anyone not standing directly in front of it. "Now. Champagne."

Flutes appeared as if the house had produced them from its bones. Susan held her glass at the centre of the table; Henry lifted his; Ed raised his, eyes warm. Ed seemed unaware of the fact Lucy was slightly uncomfortable. Lucy followed suit.

"To Edward and Lucy," Susan said. "To a beautiful wedding, and a happy life."

"Hear hear!" Henry yelled, too loud. Susan shot a disapproving look in his direction.

Lucy sipped the champagne, the bubbles seeming to sting. "Thank you. It was..." She faltered, looking for the right word. "Perfect, really." She let herself remember the candlelight, the string quartet, the way Ed had looked at her during the vows, as though everything that had happened before and after were no more than scenery. She clung to that look like a good-luck charm.

"Perfect," Susan echoed. "Yes. The photographs came through yesterday. We've chosen a few for the mantel. The one of you signing the register is very sweet." *Sweet* somehow took on a hard edge. "I'm glad you decided to wear your hair up in the end, even after all that adorable hesitation."

She says "adorable" like it's a weakness. Lucy smoothed a stray imaginary hair at her nape. She needed to get out of her head, but she somehow doubted necking her champagne in one would go down well.

She had worn it up because Susan had said the neckline of the dress demanded it. What mother-in-law wanted, mother-in-law got.

"Shall I carve?" Henry spoke as if afraid of his wife's reaction.

"Please," Susan said. "And don't be stingy. Edward eats like a farmhand, even now."

"Occupational hazard." Ed grinned. "Law makes a man hungry."

"It makes a man something," Susan said, and the room laughed obediently. Lucy resisted the urge to point out that didn't really mean anything.

Susan served the plates with the air of a woman doling out alms. The beef blushed in the middle; the roast potatoes cracked, promising their centres. Lucy picked up her knife and fork and remembered to keep her elbows off the table. She remembered the voice in her head that had been with her since the engagement.

Be gracious; be bright; do not try too hard but try hard enough.

"So," Susan said, after the first appreciative mouthfuls, "how is school, Lucy?"

"It's going well," Lucy said. "We've started a new reading scheme and it's already... helping." She could hear herself slipping into teacher mode and pulled back. "The children are sweet. Exhausting. But sweet."

"Exhausting," Susan repeated, nodding. "That is the appropriate word for it, in my view. I don't know how you do it. All that noise." She dabbed at the corner of her mouth, set the napkin down, and gave a practised smile. "Still, someone has to. It's a calling, isn't it? Teaching. Vocational."

Lucy knew the script when she heard it. Vocational meant noble, which meant underpaid, which meant not quite the sort of thing one would choose if one could choose anything. She let the barb drift past.

"I love it," she said. "They say the most unexpected things. You never get two days the same."

Henry leaned forward, eyes glassy, licking his lips before he spoke. "Do you still teach handwriting?"

"We call it 'handwriting and fine motor,' now."

"Modern names," Henry said. "Everything needs to sound new these days. Same story, different pens, eh?"

"Pencils," Lucy said, smiling. "We only graduate to pens when they're ready."

"Ah," Henry said, looking longingly at the bottle of champagne.

Susan's fork chimed on china, once, precise. "And you're

enjoying the house?" she asked, as though the house might be a temperamental relative Lucy was hoping to win over.

"We are," Lucy said quickly. "It's beautiful. We're very grateful."

Ed reached for her hand under the table. A quiet pulse, a code. *We're fine. You're doing fine.* She wanted to believe him. She was relieved he'd finally noticed howe tough this was.

"The garden," Susan muttered. "It needs management. Edward never was one for pruning."

"I'll learn," Lucy said, though she had always killed houseplants with too much love and not enough light.

"You will," Susan said, and made it both blessing and verdict.

For a while they ate. The conversation moved through weather (the old British classic), travel (the parents' cruise booked for December, "just before Christmas, so as not to miss the family day itself"), and neighbours (Mrs Tennant's hip, poor dear). Lucy contributed at the edges, careful, the way you step along a wet kerb. Each time she allowed herself to relax, she found a new code she didn't understand: a glance between Susan and Henry at the mention of "traditions," a small tightening around Susan's mouth when Ed mentioned a university friend. History, an invisible but real presence in the room, as much a part of the table as the silver.

"And the honeymoon?" Susan asked. "We've only seen a handful of photographs."

"It was lovely," Lucy said. "Devon. Quiet." She had wanted Italy, then agreed to Devon because Ed had been snowed under with a trial. In truth, the idea of slipping away close to home, just the two of them, had sounded romantic in a very English way. Cottages and rain and bread left on the step by a neighbour with a note: *Welcome, newlyweds.* "We walked a lot," she added. "Clifftops. The wind practically lifted us off."

"You've always liked the sea," Henry said to Ed, with the tone of a man not certain he could rely on his memory. It was almost a question.

"Still do," Ed said. "We'll get back there. Won't we, Luce?"

"We will," Lucy said, and meant it.

Susan set down her knife with a heavy noise, as if she was troubled that she had suddenly stopped being the centre of attention. "And children. I suppose that question is allowed now, yes? When might we expect to be grandparents?"

Lucy kept her expression neutral. She had practised this in the bathroom: how not to flinch, how not to look at Ed, how not to be caught in a trap.

"We're not in a rush," she said. "We're still enjoying being newlyweds."

"How novel," Susan said. "But it's good to be practical. Wouldn't you agree? There's timing to consider. Men are blessed with the luxury of indecision. We, my dear, are not. *Tick tock, tick tock*, you understand?" Her lips became thin for one judgemental moment. "How old are you now, darling?"

Lucy made her sip of water look like the kind of sip a calm woman takes. "Thirty."

"Thirty," Susan repeated. "One can't say you have *plenty* of time, of course, but your clock hasn't quite run out." There was a pause in which Lucy waited for Ed to say something, the thing a husband might say in his wife's defence. There was nothing.

"Edward was such a gorgeous baby," Susan went on. "It would be a delight to see another. Though of course, these things are really up to the woman, aren't they?"

Henry cleared his throat, half-heartedly, attempting to get his wife's attention but too afraid to go the whole hog. *These people are like goddamn puppets to her.*

"We'll let you know when there's news," Ed said tightly, not quite meeting anyone's eyes. It was something, at least.

"Of course," Susan said, as if he'd agreed to a delivery slot. "I only mean... family is everything, in the end. We've always said so. Traditions. Continuity."

The word "nursery" ached in Lucy's mind; she buried it. "I understand. And I agree. Family matters."

"I'm so glad," Susan murmured. "You've settled so beautifully into everything. I must say, we were a little... surprised at first. It all happened rather quickly, didn't it? But then, when you know, you know."

It had been quick. A meeting at a fundraiser for the school, Ed's firm sponsoring new laptops, a PR event that had turned into a surprisingly easy conversation, then a drink, then a dinner, then winter walks that felt like secret adventures only they could understand the significance of. She remembered those days as a contrast of winter cold against his physical heat. Kisses in the rain. Clinging desperately to each other as a fire raged in their getaway cottage. As winter turned to spring, Ed popped the question.

Lucy held her glistening ring up for examination now and made herself look exactly as sorry as the room apparently required. "We were lucky."

"Luck favours the organised," Susan said. "If you weren't ready for love, your heart wouldn't have opened. Don't you agree?"

The question wasn't a question; Susan didn't expect a response.

"Speaking of organised," Henry murmured, his cheeks red either from embarrassment or too much drink. Or both. "Edward, I meant to ask about that case—"

"Not at lunch, Henry," Susan said, sweet as arsenic. "Lucy doesn't want shop talk. Do you, dear?"

"I don't mind," Lucy said honestly. She could talk about anything that wasn't her womb.

"Later," Susan decided. That was enough to shut Henry up.

Ed caught Lucy's eye then, and there it was again finally. The look from the wedding, a gentle but almost reluctant apology. He was trying, she knew. He was always trying to stand between the old world and the new, to make excuses for his mother while hoping Lucy would accept her hard edges.

"Tell us about your parents," Susan said. "I was so disappointed when they couldn't make the wedding. You can tell a lot about who a woman will become by studying her mother." She glanced at Henry, then at Ed, as if realising her mistake. "Not so much with fathers and sons, I fear."

"Mum had a chest infection," Lucy said. "Dad decided to stay behind to help her deal with it." She didn't say that her mother had felt out of place long before the day, imagining the Keatons in their pearls and certainty, deciding not to be measured at all because she believed, or perhaps knew, she could never match them. "They're hoping to come up before Christmas," Lucy added quickly. "To see the house."

"How lovely. We'll have them for drinks. We must all be... pleasant and merry, mustn't we?"

"That would be nice." Lucy pictured her mother on one of these chairs, her father counting the forks, and felt loyalty prickle.

We are not inferior to you.

"Edward's sister will be back by then, with any luck," Henry said, almost to himself, as if to slip the sentence past Susan's guard.

A small pause. Susan's rictus smile twitched slightly. It looked almost painful.

"Perhaps," she said. "We'll see. It depends what her schedule permits."

Lucy kept her face trained. In the weeks since the wedding she had learned that Josephine was a prickly topic of conversation. As if the speaker would be harmed by talking about her. As if a listener would be somehow and vaguely offended.

She was abroad. Busier than most people would understand. Unwell once, but better now. A scattering of stories that didn't coalesce into a single picture.

The talk softened when Susan served dessert. Apple tart with a gloss like a shop window. Susan told a story about Ed as a boy, falling asleep under the table at Christmas with a paper crown sliding down his face. Lucy laughed in the right places, and, for a moment, almost enjoyed it: the ritual of Sunday, the sense that she was in the photograph rather than looking at it.

"Coffee?" Susan said, after Henry had insisted on seconds then declared himself quite undone. "Edward, darling, be useful."

Ed stood. "Of course."

Lucy half-rose. "Let me help."

"Nonsense." Susan placed her hand on Lucy's shoulder with a small rustle of authority. "Sit. You're our guest."

"I thought I was family," Lucy said, trying to make her tone jokey.

"Both," Susan said, no humour, no joke, dead and flat and borderline sadistic. "For now."

For now?

The clock in the hall took struck the hour like Susan's personal backing track. Through the window, a gust of wind combed the copper leaves into a different pattern. Ed left for the kitchen and Henry tipped his glass, searching for the last drop.

Susan folded her hands on the tablecloth as if beginning a meeting. "You are doing beautifully," she said. "Truly. It's not easy, assimilating."

Lucy blinked. "Assimilating?"

"Into a family with... established ways. We value steadiness. Loyalty. We protect our own."

"I value those things too," Lucy said, wondering where her mother-in-law was going with this.

"Good," Susan said. "Then we won't have any trouble, will we?"

Before Lucy could ask what sort of trouble, and what the consequences would be, and exactly what they were talking about, Ed returned with a tray. He set mugs down. The coffee was strong enough for an all-nighter marking papers. Susan took hers black. Henry poured from a silver mug of milk until beads slid down the side. Lucy curled her hands around the heat of the mug and let it seep into her.

"You'll find your rhythm," Susan said, lifting her mug. "Just do what you've been doing. Smile. Keep the home gentle. Let Edward be... Edward." She made it sound like both instruction and benediction. "Children will come when they come. Or they won't. Either way, we adjust. We're very good at making things look as they should."

There it was again, the pretend casual attitude when it came to children, but Susan couldn't hide the tightness in her tone. And Lucy couldn't stop an icy finger from shivering up her spine.

~

The coffee was still warm in Lucy's hands when the sound split the house. A slam. Sharp, rattling the glass in the doors as if the house itself flinched.

All four of them froze. The longcase clock marked the silence with a tick that sounded suddenly too loud. Then came footsteps: firm, confident, heels striking the polished wood of the hall with a rhythm that belonged to someone who did not need permission to be here.

Susan's cup paused midway to her lips. Her face paled, the

colour slipping away. Henry studied the tablecloth, his hand circling the rim of his glass as though the answer to the noise lay in the dregs of wine. He looked at his champagne glass as if maybe the answer was there instead, then gazed around for more booze.

Ed rose from his chair. His eyes shone in a way Lucy hadn't seen in weeks, maybe months. Not relief, not exactly joy, something sharper, more immediate.

The door swung wide and there she stood. The prodigal daughter.

Josephine.

Suitcase in one hand, red lipstick painted with purpose, a black coat falling open to show a blouse too fine for travel. Her red hair flowed to her shoulders, fiery and undeniably beautiful.

She stood framed in the doorway for a beat, knowing exactly how long it takes to make an entrance. There was something fake about her.

"Darling." Her voice was low, warm, unhurried, made for late-night confidences and secrets whispered in alcoves.

Ed crossed the room in three strides. He didn't hesitate. He didn't ask why she was here. He folded her in, arms tight around her waist, her head buried against his chest. She held on too long. Her eyes were open over his shoulder, scanning the room like a queen greeting her subjects, deciding which were loyal and which were disposable.

Susan set down her mug carefully, the porcelain sound precise as a scalpel. Her hands were steady, but that milky paleness had only become more pronounced. Henry cleared his throat into his napkin, eyes fixed on the table as though he might disappear into it.

At last Josephine released Ed, though not entirely. Her hand lingered on his arm, fingers pressing into his sleeve, a private code in plain sight. Then she turned to Lucy with her hand possessively upon her husband. It was like a challenge.

"You must be the wife."

The wife. Not *Lucy*. Not even *Ed's wife*. The wife. A category. A placeholder.

Lucy forced her a smile, though it felt brittle on her lips. "Yes. And you must be Josephine. It's lovely to finally—"

"Meet?" Josephine tilted her head. "Yes. I suppose it is."

Josephine set her suitcase down and stepped further in, owning the space. Lucy felt like one of the quiet girls she taught, the ones who retreated to the library at lunchtime and always pretended they were okay. "Ed's told me almost nothing about you. Where are you from? What do you do? Do you have family?"

The questions came one after another, relentless, like opening salvos in a battle.

"I grew up in Wiltshire. I'm a primary school teacher."

"No brothers or sisters?" Josephine said *just* before Lucy was done speaking. She was marking her territory.

"No. I'm an only child."

Josephine's mouth curved, though it wasn't quite a smile. "How lonely."

The words hurt somehow, like a hand pressed where a bruise hadn't healed.

Lucy shifted in her chair, felt her dress rustling against her skin, feeling the air close in. "Not really. I had friends."

"Of course," Josephine said smoothly, her gaze sliding back to her brother. "And Ed."

"I didn't know Ed when I was a child."

"No, no, of course not. But the universe knew you would end up together, did it not? Is that not the nature of love?"

Lucy tried to sip her coffee, but her hand shook, and she set the cup down too quickly, the spoon rattling in the saucer. She was beginning to get sick of pretending the nonsense these people spouted made any sense.

She remembered what she'd been told: Josephine lived abroad. Josephine was working. Josephine couldn't make the wedding because of commitments that simply couldn't be changed. All neat, plausible reasons. So why was she here now, without warning, walking into the dining room as if she had never left?

Lucy's eyes drifted down to the suitcase. It wasn't large. A small bag, really. Hardly enough for a long stay. Just enough to say: *I'm here. I belong. I don't need to explain.*

She smiled again, brittle, and wondered – not for the first time – what exactly she had married into. This family didn't look like they were welcoming a daughter home. It was more like they were bracing themselves for a storm.

2

October 19th

The light had thinned by the time plates were nudged back into place and the conversation found a shape again. The roast beef had cooled to a comfortable warmth; the gravy had grown a skin. Josephine sat beside Edward, close enough that the sleeve of her black coat brushed his cuff whenever she lifted her glass.

"Don't let me interrupt," Josephine said, which was ludicrous considering her Broadway-esque entrance. She took the seat opposite Ed immediately. Lucy was conscious of her husband aiming his attention fully at his sister, giving Lucy the ice-cold shoulder. Josephine tipped her head, the red of her lipstick catching the room's glow. "Finish your coffee Tell me everything I've missed."

Nobody quite knew where to begin. Susan's smile fixed and held. Henry retreated an inch deeper into his glass. Ed, energised in a way Lucy hadn't seen since the wedding, leaned toward his sister. The years seemed to fold in on themselves until the pair of them were sitting at a smaller table, in a smaller house, talking in a language only the two of them remembered. Ed spoke with quick passion about his latest case, then they moved onto their childhood.

"Do you remember the summer the river flooded?" Josephine said. "We built a raft out of pallets and bailer twine. You swore it would float." She tutted at Susan. "Mother, a coffee, please?"

Susan stood abruptly and began pouring her a mug.

"It did float," Ed said, laughing, seeming to miss the strange exchange. Or maybe it was only strange for Lucy. "For six minutes."

"Five," she returned, eyes alight. "I timed it. You insisted we should try again because Robinson Crusoe would never have given up, and I told you Robinson Crusoe had a writer to keep him alive."

Ed's laugh was softer now, fond and unembarrassed. "You always had a line ready."

"I always had to," Josephine said, her voice edged with something Lucy couldn't name.

Lucy tried to include herself into their easy flow. "It sounds... lovely," she said, and heard how weak the word sounded. "I bet you were a pair of terrors." She was speaking with her family, so why then did she feel like she was auditioning?

"We were a *team*," Josephine said with emphasis. "Us against the world. Weren't we, Ed?"

"We were," he said, and Lucy, who was newly in the business of decoding micro-expressions, noticed the small, apologetic glance he cast her way, as if to say: *it's not about you; it was just how it was.*

Susan cleared her throat, hostess again. "Henry, darling, more champagne?"

Henry nodded, morose, none of the alcoholic excitement Lucy had expected. "You know I can't turn down a drink."

"Anybody else?" Susan said.

"Not for me," Josephine muttered, looking at Lucy out of the corner of her eye.

"I'm fine, thank you," Lucy lied. Something in her sister-in-law's expression made drinking seem wrong.

"Do you remember Mrs Gillingham's tarts?" she said, eyes flicking to Ed. "Saturday afternoons. We'd wait by the hedge like little thieves."

"You stole jam tarts?" Lucy tried again, lighter this time. "Were you ever caught?"

Josephine turned slowly, as if the sound had only just reached her. "Oh, you wouldn't really get it I suppose, would you?" she said, almost affectionate. "Being an only child."

Lucy wanted to slap her. It was beyond rude. Nobody said anything, nobody stood up for her, and Lucy found she couldn't stand up for herself. "I suppose not. But I can imagine."

"Can you?" Josephine's smile bent a fraction. "Imagining isn't the same as knowing."

Ed aimed a half-hearted warning glance at his sister, but it arrived as fondness instead. It was a look that said: *Oh, you do take things a tad too far sometimes, but you're an angel, nonetheless.*

Susan put her napkin down and picked it back up again. "Josie," she said with careful brightness, "Lucy was just telling us about the school's new reading scheme. The children are thriving."

Lucy was grateful for the support but also confused. Why was her mother-in-law suddenly being nice to her? It was like one predator warning another not to get carried away.

"Children thrive if you give them respect," Josephine replied, not looking at Lucy at all. "And if you tell them stories that make the dark tolerable Though, making the dark *in*tolerable has a charm of its own." She smiled at Ed. "We used to terrify each other with stories, didn't we? That the bull in Mr

Conway's field could smell fear, and that the well by the lane had no bottom."

"You said if anyone fell in, they'd keep falling until they forgot their name."

"I said *you* would keep falling until you forgot *my* name," Josephine corrected. "So, you wouldn't love me anymore. And then I cried until you promised never to go near the well."

Henry, who had been stubbornly sipping champagne, tried a diversion. "We should take you both to the new exhibition at the city gallery. Landscapes. Old ones. Very soothing."

"Art should set your teeth on edge," Josephine said dismissively. "Or what's the point?"

Susan's voice cooled by a degree. "Not everything must be a trial, darling. Some things can simply be... pleasant."

"Pleasant," Josephine repeated, scowling at her mother as it to ask how she dared to use that tone with her. "Speaking of pleasant..." She glanced at Ed, then at her parents, then finally, lazily, at Lucy. "I've quit. Work. The whole thing. Dreadful job. Dreadful people. Fresh start."

Susan's eyebrows shot up. "When did you decide?"

"Last month," Josephine said. "Don't look at me like that. Change is good."

"Where were you?" Lucy asked, keeping the tone light, the question small enough to be polite... she hoped. "Ed said Barcelona, but that you travelled. Were you based in Spain, then?"

"Among other places. I floated." She twirled a hand. "Here and there."

Oh, I am so impressed. You are not of this earth, ye great one.

"And you're back for how long?" Lucy asked, praying the answer was a day. Which was a petty thought, but one she had anyway. "Will you be based here now?" The question came out too blunt.

"I'm home," Josephine said simply. "I'll stay with Mum and Dad for a bit. They'll be so glad to have me." She tilted her head at Susan, who folded her hands too neatly on her napkin. A look passed between parent and daughter, swift as a wire pulled taut and released.

Ed cleared his throat. "It'll be good to have you around. For a while."

"For a while," Josephine echoed. "It sounds as if you want me to leave."

Ed winked at her. "Don't be so silly. You were always so sensitive."

Susan tried again to reroute the current. "Josie, why don't you tell Lucy about the year you spent in France when you were nineteen? The language school. The—"

"That was years ago," Josephine said, with a small, amused sigh. Another absurdity. She had wanted to talk about the past ever since she'd got here. "No one cares about my verbs, Mother."

"I do," Henry said. "I always liked the way you said *bonjour*. Sounded like you meant it."

Josephine's eyes warmed for a split second, then cooled as she pivoted back to Lucy. "What was your wedding like?" she asked, as if the question had just occurred to her. "I saw some pictures. You looked... sweet."

Lucy felt her cheeks heat. "It was small. Family. Friends."

"I would have come. But work was impossible then. Flights, commitments, the usual." She speared a carrot. "You know how it is. The flying never stops for a highflier. God, I'm glad to be rid of it. Glad to be home."

"I don't, actually," Lucy said lightly. "Term dates are pretty regular."

"Oh, well, it's nice for some," Josephine said.

Lucy pretended not to hear the stinging resentment in her voice.

The stories kept coming. Ed remembered the time he fell from the barn roof trying to impress her; Josephine remembered telling him he fell out of love with gravity before he hit the ground. They laughed like – and this was a cruel, secret thought – *lovers* at that. They described a winter school play in which she had been the moon, and he had been a tree; how she had shone, and he had held her up with his branches. They folded themselves into the past with such ease that Lucy felt superfluous in the present.

She tried to anchor the conversation in facts. "So, you've been away... how many years is it now?"

Josephine's eyes flicked, sharp as a blade. "Why? Do you need to pin me to a calendar, Lucy?"

"Nuh-no," Lucy said. *Why is she so confrontational?* "I'm curious."

"I moved around," Josephine said. "Here and there, there and here. It's not a crime."

"Jo," Ed said gently.

Josephine's expression softened. "It doesn't matter," she said to him, dismissing Lucy without looking at her. "I'm here now."

Lucy heard what wasn't being said. She pressed the heel of her hand under the table into the seam of the cloth.

The light lowered itself another notch, and the room obliged, becoming intimate. Josephine told a story about a bonfire night when a spark had landed on her sleeve and Ed had beaten it out with his hands; she told another about a day the headmistress had called their mother because Josephine had bloodied the nose of a boy who had called Ed names. She smiled as she told it, and Lucy noticed how the smile didn't quite reach her eyes.

"Violence doesn't suit you," Susan said.

"Oh, Mum," Josephine said softly. "It suited me fine. I can't say the same for the bully though. Speaking of things suiting me, can I assume I still have a place here?"

"We'll make space," Susan said, so quietly Lucy almost missed it. It wasn't an invitation. It was a concession.

Lucy had never been good at leaving threads dangling. "What will you do?" she asked, listening to her own voice for any sign of accusation and finding none. Only curiosity, and a fear she could not name. "Workwise, I mean."

"Oh, this and that." Josephine's eyes glittered as if she were auctioning herself off to the highest bidder in the room. "Something that fits."

Susan rose with decisive grace, skimming a hand over the cloth the way a pianist closes a lid. "Well. That was lovely. Henry, come and look at those letters I mentioned." She turned to Josephine. "We'll speak later."

"Of course," Josephine said, and for the first time since she'd arrived, she looked at her mother with the face of a child.

They left, Susan hurrying, Henry trailing behind like a loyal dog. For a beat no one spoke. Lucy began to gather the plates for clearing away because that was what a person did when they didn't know what else to do.

"You don't need to do that," Josephine said with disgust. "Mummy will handle it."

Ed must've finally realised, or acknowledged, that this was simply horrible for Lucy. He put his hands on his hips and said, "Well, we better be off."

About bloody time.

"Oh, really?" Josephine said. "I've travelled so far."

"We'll see each other soon."

"Will we, Eddy? Really?"

Lucy stood and almost yanked Ed to his feet. She felt like insects were crawling over her skin.

At the door, Josephine turned her face to Ed and kissed his cheek. It was a sister's kiss and not a sister's kiss. Her hand stayed on his arm a heartbeat too long, thumb pressing a small, deliberate circle into the fabric.

"I'll see you very soon," she said, just for him.

"Soon," he echoed dully. Her husband sounded like a well-trained pet, and she hated it.

"How soon?" Josephine asked.

Ed glanced between them. "Dinner next week? The three of us?"

Josephine's gaze flicked to Lucy, not unkind, but measuring, as if she were deciding which shelf to place her. "Of course," she said, as if she were doing them both a favour.

Lucy stepped out onto the gravel, the tiny stones making that somehow wealthy sound underfoot. The wind moved through the copper leaves and drew the smell of rain from the hedges. She could feel Josephine's presence behind her even when she refused to turn.

Before she reached the car, she allowed herself a glance back.

Josephine stood framed by the doorway's golden square, the hall light behind her making a small crown of her hair. She didn't wave. She didn't call after them. She only looked, and the look was a claim laid on something Lucy had thought was already hers.

The smile didn't fade.

Not when Lucy opened the passenger door. Not when Ed started the engine and the radio stuttered to life to some polite string concerto. Not when the car rolled past the front hedge and the house retreated into the picturesqueness that other people admired from the lane.

The smile followed them, lodged in Lucy's brain like a shard of glass.

"She's... intense," Lucy said, aiming for airy and missing by a mile.

"She's Josie," Ed said, as if that explained everything.

Lucy looked straight ahead at the road that cut the afternoon into obedient pieces. She tried to translate what had happened into a language she knew. She tried to write herself back into the centre of her own life.

3

October 28th

A few days later, the sting of the lunch had begun to fade. Just.

By the time Lucy drove around the corner to home, the grey sky had lowered itself over the street like a lid. Wet pavements held the day's bruised light; a dog had left small signatures in the slick that ran along the curb. Lucy parked up and let herself into the front gate, mind already sifting through spellings tests, a note from a parent who did not like the new phonics, and whether they had any milk left.

The front door was not only unlocked; it was ajar.

She reached out, the brass cold under her fingers, and nudged it wider. "Ed?" she called, though she was sure he'd still be at work.

Garlic and onions came first, then something deeper beneath: meat, thyme, the tempting pull of gravy. The radio was playing, a presenter chuckling.

"Hello?" she said, getting worried now. *Yeah, Luce, because somebody's broken in just to turn on the bloody radio and make some dinner.*

"Hi!" Josephine's answer was cheerful enough to make cheerfulness suspect. "In here."

Lucy set her school bag down carefully, as if a sudden movement might make the situation worse. She stepped through to the kitchen.

Josephine had rolled her sleeves to the elbow. A tea towel Lucy didn't recognise hung from the oven handle like a flag of occupation. Groceries Lucy hadn't bought stood at attention along the counter: a stout bag of Maris Pipers powdered with earth; a brick of cheddar sweating under plastic; a bottle of Worcestershire sauce; a pot of beef stock paste; carrots lined like recruits; a bunch of thyme held together with an elastic band. Steam beaded the window. The hob wore a sheen of splatter.

"Ed said I could stay for a while," Josephine said. "I thought I'd make myself useful." She returned to the pan with the intimacy of someone who already knew which burner ran hot and which sulked. It seemed she thought that was the end of the matter.

"That's... kind." Her pulse found a new rhythm in her throat, hard and high. "When did you—did he—"

"He messaged earlier," Josephine said, giving the onions a precise, professional stir. "I was nearby. Thought I'd surprise you both. There's nothing worse than coming home and wondering what to do about dinner, is there?" She tilted the pan, coaxed the glossy brown into the corners. "Mum's recipe. Well, hers and mine. Evolution." A handful of finely chopped carrots went in with a hush. "Cottage pie."

Cottage pie. Simple. Efficient. Comfort marching in neat squares. Lucy's was always too dry.

Josephine reached for the Worcestershire sauce. "Ed favourite," she said, without looking up. "Always was."

"Was it?" Lucy said, thinking of all the times he'd bravely soldiered through hers.

"Yes… of course. You knew that. Obviously."

"Obviously."

A small quiet arranged itself between the clink of wooden spoon on enamel and the radio's laughter. The revelation did something complicated under Lucy's ribs. She had learned a thousand things about Ed in the quick, generous months: the instant coffee he took at three in the afternoon, the way he turned his pillow in the night to find the cool again, the scar at his hairline from a childhood swing.

Favourite. Of course he had a favourite. Of course it had a name. Of course, the person who said it out loud now was not Lucy.

"Mash in a bit," Josephine said, sliding the pan off the heat to let the onions rest in their own sweetness. "Where do you keep your masher?"

"In the second drawer," Lucy said automatically, then wished she'd said nowhere, lied and said they didn't have one. Josephine opened the second drawer without hesitation and produced the masher like a magician with a hat trick.

"Perfect." She moved with the efficiency of someone who had cooked in this room. "You look knackered. Sit. Do you want a glass of wine?" She had already half-turned toward the rack.

"No," Lucy said, too quickly. *I want you out of my house.* "Thank you. I need the toilet."

"Down the hall on the left," Josephine said, oh-so accommodating.

"Yes, thank you. I know where my toilet is."

In the downstairs loo Lucy shut the door and leaned her forehead against the cool mirror for a count of three, then another. She pulled out her mobile, pressed Edward's name; it rang twice, three times, four.

He answered on the fifth with a smile in his voice. "Nearly home."

"Ed." She swallowed, struggled to find a calm tone. "Josephine is here."

"Yeah?" Relief poured down the line. "Good."

"She's cooking. In our kitchen. She's bought a new tea towel."

"That's nice of her."

"She said you told her she could stay."

Either Lucy was terrible at being passive aggressive, or Ed was missing the point.

"I did. I should have called. I assumed—I mean—I thought you'd be fine."

"I wasn't expecting her," Lucy said. "In our house, Ed. The door was... open."

It didn't sound as ominous as it had somehow felt.

"She's my sister," he said, rushing to do what love always does in families: excuse, explain, erase. "She's had a rough time. She needs us. Just for a bit."

"How long is a *bit*?" She didn't mean for the words to sound like a test, but there they were, sat up straight in their school chairs.

"Let's just get through tonight." His voice softened. "I've missed her."

I've missed you, Lucy almost said, but she wasn't sure what that even meant.

"I'm almost home," he went on. "Try to relax. It's dinner, not a tribunal."

She ended the call and pressed the heel of her hand under her ribs until the ache steadied, washed her hands as if she'd been out in mud, then returned to her kitchen.

Josephine was putting potatoes into a pan. "I'll mash these with butter and cheddar," she said. "And a little mustard. Mum swears by milk; I swear by cream. Don't tell her. Or do." She hummed a little childlike tune. "Ed will be thrilled."

The implication was, Lucy felt, that she didn't know how to thrill her own husband.

The radio murmured something pleasant about traffic on the ring road; Josephine reached to turn it down. "Tell me about your day," she said, owning not just the kitchen, but the conversation too. "Any little geniuses?"

Lucy perched on the edge of a chair, uncomfortable, aware of the ridiculousness of perching in your own kitchen. "They're learning 'because'," she said. "Half of them spell it B-E-C-O-S on instinct. I'm trying to teach them the logic—be-cause—two words stitched—" She stopped when she saw the patronising look on Josephine's face. "Nothing interesting."

"You shouldn't be so shy. We're at home. Relax."

You're in MY home, Lucy thought. *There's a serious difference.*

Lucy shifted. "I'm not being shy. Or anything."

"Has anybody ever told you that you can be the teensy bit prickly?"

Before Lucy could answer, the front door clicked; Edward's keys made their habitual jangle in the saucer by the stairs; his step found the squeaky note in the floorboard. He came into the doorway with his tie yanked half loose and something like relief lit across his face when he saw the two of them in the kitchen. He looked relieved that they hadn't taken chunks out of each other.

"That smells incredible," he said, and crossed to kiss Lucy, neat and correct, then hugged his sister, less neat, fiercer. "You didn't have to—"

"I wanted to," Josephine cut in. "Cottage pie. Your favourite And I tidied your spice cupboard. You had three jars of cumin and no Paprika." Lucy glanced at the cupboard and felt invaded on a molecular level.

"We had a system," she muttered.

Josephine aimed that patronising look again. "Now you have a better one."

Ed laughed. He looked ten years younger when he was with his sister.

Don't be bitter, she thought... bitterly.

"I'm going to grab a quick shower before dinner," Lucy said.

"Oh, sure." Ed didn't look at her.

She made the shower last a long, long time, then read her book for a while before Josephine called her down.

~

The pie came out perfect, the edges were crisp and proud, the middle was a soft, savoury cloud. Ed said "God" around the first mouthful. Lucy buried the mean observation that his tone was husky and excited like he got during sex.

Josephine set down stories like courses: the time they had faked a fever, mouths flushed with hot water and cheeks pinched, to skip school and build a fort under the table; the summer they had slept in the garden on a mattress and woken soaked in dew; the day Ed had bloodied his knee and she had torn a strip from her dress to bind it. Ed fed details into the tales like seasoning. The two of them glowed under their own nostalgia.

"Lucy probably thinks our family is a bit much for her," Josephine said at one point, not unkind, but with the theatrical generosity of someone who has already decided your lines for you.

Ed gave an awkward laugh and didn't quite meet Lucy's eyes. "We can be... intense," he allowed.

"We can be loyal," Josephine corrected. "Which is a relief, in a world like this."

Lucy swallowed. "I think family is wonderful. I'm glad you're close."

A long look from the Sister of the Year, derisive and disbelieving, until she finally graced Lucy with the gift of speech. "So are we."

Lucy tried to talk about the wedding then. She took the story out carefully, like something soft and shining from tissue paper. "Since you weren't there," she said, "you'll enjoy this. The vicar did that bit I love, about love not boasting and keeping no record of wrongs. The flowers were white and blue—"

"Sweet," she Josephine interrupted. "Mum sent me the photos. You looked... happy?"

We were happy. We are happy. Full stop.

"I was," Lucy said, and held Josephine's gaze. "We are."

"Of course," Josephine murmured, and sprinkled a bright shower of salt over her plate as if seasoning the sentence.

After, they all cleaned up as if they were a neat little family. Josephine washed, Ed dried, Lucy cleaned the surfaces, as if their roles had been written months or years ago.

In the living room, Josephine sat without asking where anyone usually sat. She chose Lucy's corner – the corner with the sun in late morning and the throw she'd bought in a burst of optimism the week they moved in – curled into it and tucked her feet under her, an annoyingly elegant trespasser.

Lucy hesitated in the doorway for a breath then crossed to the armchair instead, as if this were a rearrangement they'd discussed and agreed upon. Ed dropped onto the sofa, the space between himself and his sister the width of a cushion and no more.

"Before we get comfy, would anybody like some tea?" Lucy asked.

"Please," Josephine said, switching on the television and flicking between channels. "Two sugars."

Lucy stood restlessly. In the kitchen, she braced her hands on the counter and let the kettle fill the silence. She turned the pot on the draining board and considered throwing it away just to decide someone else hadn't made first.

When she brought the mugs through, Josephine accepted hers without looking at or acknowledging Lucy.

Maybe you'd prefer it all over that frustratingly beautiful red hair of hours.

The TV audience laughed at the canned sitcom humour; the siblings laughed with them and Lucy didn't find it funny.

During the ad break, Josephine shifted closer to Ed, thigh brushing thigh in the thoughtless way families allowed themselves... right? That was all it was, all Lucy could let it be. "Do you remember when the power went out that winter and we all slept in the sitting room?" she said. "Dad made a fire, and you told me stories until I fell asleep."

Ed smiled at the memory and for a second Lucy saw the shape of him at twelve. He reached for the throw and tucked it around Josephine's knees, a small, absent, devastating kindness.

Lucy looked down at her mug. She told herself that this was the first evening. That first evenings are always ugly and awkward. That tomorrow the door would be locked the way it always had been when she got home; that the drawer would contain its old, imperfect system; that Josephine would catch a bus to her parents' and Ed would cover Lucy's cold legs with the throw instead.

Josephine glanced over. "You're very quiet."

"I'm watching," Lucy said, which was true, just not about the television.

"You'll get used to us," Josephine said.

Lucy didn't want to get used to whatever this was. She said nothing.

Ed turned the volume up a notch. Once the sitcom was over, he said, "This film looks all right. Who fancies it?"

"Me!" Josephine exclaimed.

The film was a boring World War Two drama, not Lucy's kind of thing at all, but she wasn't going to be outdone. "It looks absolutely sensational," she said dryly.

As they watched, Lucy sat lonely in the armchair and the super siblings cuddled closer and closer. It was a relief when the shooting finally stopped, and the credits rolled.

Josephine stretched with catlike grace. "I should get my things. Where shall I..."

"Spare room," Ed said, already up, as if he were the concierge in a hotel where courtesy had long ago become instinct.

Lucy carried the mugs into the kitchen to get some space from them. She opened the back door and sucked in the fresh air desperately. The garden was slick and quiet and privately hers in a way the house was not tonight.

When she went back in, Josephine and Ed were coming down the stairs, talking in a shorthand made of old jokes and a geography Lucy had never learned.

"Goodnight," Josephine said to Lucy, that faint, deliberate smile back in place. "Thank you for dinner."

"You cooked it," Lucy said.

"I mean thank you for the company," Josephine said, and it sounded like she meant: *thank you for witnessing how easily I make myself at home.*

Once Josephine had gone, Ed kissed Lucy's temple, the same spot he'd first kissed before finding her lips those too-long, too-short months ago. "You okay?"

"I'm fine," she said.

Why couldn't she just be honest? She didn't want to upset him, she told herself. No, she wasn't scared of a confrontation.

Upstairs, doors opened and closed softly.

"I'm heading up," he said. "You coming?"

"Yeah, just give me five."

Lucy stood in the middle of her living room and looked at the indentation on the sofa cushion where she usually sat. It was still warm. She reached out and pressed her hand against it.

She turned off the lamp, climbed the stairs, and paused outside the spare room where she had once kept winter coats and a box of things she hadn't wanted to unpack yet. Old photo frames, a ceramic bowl with a hairline crack, a paper bag of cables that belonged to devices long gone. The door was open half an inch, the light off, the dark full of the sound of someone else's breathing. Lucy placed her palm against the wood and felt, for a wonderful and probably insane moment, the warmth of the house gather under her hand as if it belonged to her after all.

In bed, Ed found her hand under the duvet. "Thank you," he whispered. "For being so understanding."

Lucy couldn't let this situation slip by any longer. She took a breath, then asked, "How long is she staying?"

"A while," he said sleepily. "We'll figure it out."

I've already figured it out. Make her leave.

All too soon, her husband was sleeping. Lucy felt exhausted, but also flooded with adrenaline, urging her to act.

In the morning, Lucy told herself, she would claim the small things back, the drawer, her spot on the sofa. She would ask Ed, no, she would *demand* that he give her a specific timeframe. She wouldn't admit defeat.

She refused to live with an intruder.

4

October 30th

Two days later and it was like the house was holding its breath. Lucy still had no timeframe, no answers. She climbed the stairs with a basket of clean laundry against her hip, thinking about spelling tests to mark, the ordinary drift of a day tugging her forward, until she reached the landing and stopped.

Josephine's door was open.

It shouldn't have meant anything. Doors open and close. Sheets dry on banisters. People get used to other people. But Lucy's body understood before her mind did. She froze in the lamplight's spill and looked in. It was a premonition, a primal feeling.

Something is wrong.

Josephine stood before the mirror, posing in one of Lucy's dresses, the green one with the soft waist and the sleeve that fell just so, the dress Ed had called "gorgeous" the night they'd gone to that little Italian and he'd laughed into his wine. The fabric sat on Josephine as if it had been made for a slightly better version of the person who owned it.

On the dressing table: Lucy's lipstick uncapped. Josephine lifted it to her mouth with the same concentration Lucy used on children's plasters and new-ink pens. The colour came to life as it met Josephine's lips. A careful swipe, a pout, a second pass.

For a moment Lucy simply watched. Two days ago, it had been cottage pie and a stolen spot on the sofa. Tonight, it was green fabric and lipstick, and an ugly question Lucy didn't want to ask but did anyway: *how exactly does a person become you?*

"We're going to The Fox and Dovecote," Josephine said to the mirror, as if Lucy had asked. "Ed texted. Everyone's meeting at eight."

Everyone. The word underlined itself. Lucy searched her memory for the conversation she must have missed. She found nothing. She mentally read the text threads with her eyes closed: Can you grab milk? Don't forget the electricity bill. See you at seven.

Nothing about Josephine. She and Ed were going for dinner to meet with some of his colleagues. Lucy hadn't known Josephine was invited.

"Take that off," Lucy said, surprising herself with the steadiness of her voice. Not a shout. Not even a tremor.

Josephine turned, slow and uninterested, the dress catching her hips as if it had fallen in love on the way down. "It's just a dress. Don't be so uptight."

"It's my dress." She shifted the laundry basket to the other hip to expel some nervous energy. "And my lipstick."

"You can have the lipstick back," Josephine said, reaching for the cap as though she meant it. "The dress is only for tonight." She smoothed the fabric, admiring the way it obeyed. "You should take it as a compliment."

The words were wrapped like a gift, ribboned in fondness, but Lucy's skin pebbled along her arms. Compliments didn't come with the faint scent of ownership. Compliments didn't stand in your doorway stealing your life.

"We're meeting Edward's colleagues," Lucy said. "I didn't know you were coming."

Josephine's smile widened a fraction, as if someone had nudged a dimmer switch. "Why wouldn't I? I'm staying with family. I'm new in town. I should meet the people who matter to him."

Lucy thought of her own first dinner with the firm the month she and Edward had started speaking about a real future. How she had practised the names; how relieved she had been when someone had asked what she taught and listened to the answer. She thought of Josephine arriving in that space wearing Lucy's clothes and Lucy's lips.

"I'd prefer you didn't wear my clothes," Lucy said.

Josephine tilted her head, considering. "You're very territorial." She said it like an anthropologist describing a charming species. "I think it suits you. Boundaries. Structure." She picked up Lucy's perfume and held it close to her wrist without spraying. "I'm almost ready."

"Ed won't like this," Lucy said, hoping it was true.

He'll be on my side about this, at least, won't he? Would he though? Lucy wasn't as certain as she would've liked to be.

Josephine laughed, a quiet, pleased sound. "Eddy will *love* this. He *always* loves when I make an effort."

Lucy set the laundry down. She wanted to say: *you can come, but not like that*. She wanted to say: *there are ways we do things in this house*. She wanted to say: *if you want to be more like me, don't steal, because I'm not a bloody thief*. Instead, she said nothing, because nothing came that didn't make her sound exactly as uptight as Josephine had accused her of being.

She turned away.

In her bedroom the wardrobe hung open, evidence of a crime. Setting down the laundry basket, she reached for the blue dress that had felt lucky once, then changed her mind and took the black.

Downstairs the hall mirror showed two women who might have been friends if they hadn't been set to opposite purposes, both in coats, both in shoes that changed how they walked, both stopping at the same moment because they saw the same thing: themselves, doubled and almost aligned, despite their different hair colours, despite Josephine having some of Ed's features. There was something too similar about them.

"You look lovely," Josephine said.

"So do you," Lucy replied. If Josephine was going to be stubborn, Lucy decided to try and play nice.

travelled together since, apparently, they were both meeting Ed.

The gastropub had repainted its door a tasteful green and hung copper lights over the bar. Ed was at a table near the back, already in conversation with the senior associate who wore expensive watches and made sure people knew it. He looked up and – there it was – the unguarded brightness Lucy had learned to love and forgive.

He stood and kissed her cheek. "You look fantastic."

For a moment, her world was bright. Then he turned to his sister and said it again in the exact same tone.

"Everyone, this is Josephine," he said, and the table offered its chorus. Hi. Lovely to meet you. We've heard so much. Josephine slid in beside Ed with the practised grace of someone who had long ago learned how to become the centre of attention.

Lucy took the chair to his other side and told herself the seating plan didn't matter.

Someone ordered olives. Someone else explained, for the

table's benefit, the chef's philosophy of local suppliers. The talk frothed and settled. Lucy waited for a moment to belong.

"I had a boy in my class today who used 'because' properly for the first time," she said, light and small, a safe anecdote held out like a biscuit. "He said, 'I was late because the rain made my shoes slow.'"

The table smiled. The senior associate said, "That's rather poetic." Ed squeezed her knee. Josephine smiled too, her head tipped as if calculating.

The first round of drinks arrived. The conversation ambled into deadlines and the temper of a particular judge and whether the new coffee machine was an improvement or heresy. Josephine placed herself neatly in each topic, not from knowledge but energy; she was overly enthusiastic, laughed loudly, clapped her hands. Nobody else seemed to find her fake.

Lucy noticed the way Ed kept turning toward his sister bursting with warmth, then turning back to Lucy with a sense of duty. She let it happen. She wished she didn't.

I'm stronger than this, aren't I?

Apparently not.

At some point Josephine touched Ed's sleeve and told yet another anecdote that had happened long before Lucy was part of their lives. "Do you remember that winter we were snowed in?" she said. "We made porridge over the fire, and you swore you could taste char in your hair for days."

Edward laughed. "You singed your fringe."

"I did," Josephine said. "Mum nearly cried."

"You turned it into a style," Ed said warmly.

Josephine's smile tilted toward Lucy. "He's easily impressed."

She means me. She means I'm easy. Slap her, Luce. Slap her now.

Lucy smiled thinly.

The mains arrived. Lucy's fish had a lemon she did not need. The conversation shifted toward stories. Josephine was good at stories, both telling and hearing them. She knew where to begin and where to hold breath. She asked questions that sounded flattering. She laughed exactly as much as each anecdote required. She brightened the room.

Later – after the wine had done its work – Josephine took Lucy's small anecdote from the beginning of the evening and held it up as if it were a jewel she had discovered herself.

"Lucy told me the sweetest thing earlier," she said. "A little boy in her class said he was late because the rain made his shoes slow." She performed the line lightly, then let a ripple of amusement ride across her face.

The table laughed; even a withdrawn wife who seemed like she wanted to be anywhere but there, who had been quiet all evening, made a small gleeful noise. Ed laughed too, a fraction too loud, his hand tapping the table. He didn't look at Lucy.

Don't they remember I told that story? She wasn't sure. Or maybe the wine had made them forget. *She's even stealing my stories, for Christ's sake.*

Lucy felt the heat climb her chest. The evening surged on. Josephine's hand rested casually on Edward's forearm. Lucy took a sip of wine and tasted nothing.

"We put a sentence on the board," she said softly, but nobody was listening. "We talked about how sometimes we say things that feel true before they're right. Get it? They liked that."

No one heard her. Or they heard and didn't care.

By pudding, Lucy had stopped trying. She might as well have not been there.

Josephine asked the partner's wife about her ceramics class and charmed her into feeling interesting; she asked the senior associate about his late mother and expressed a forensically calculated level of remorse. She spoke to the waiter the way people who have been waited on their whole lives speak when they are trying to sound like they haven't.

Ed watched her with admiration he didn't hide. Every so often he touched Lucy's knee again as if to prove he was an attentive husband.

At the end of the evening, when everybody was drinking coffee and Ed was in the bathroom, Josephine slid into Ed's seat. "You did well," she murmured, for Lucy alone.

"Did I?" Lucy said bitterly. She didn't need Josephine's approval. And yet – this was the worst part – she was grateful for it.

"Yes... considering," she said, with a pout as if to draw attention to Lucy's lipstick on her mouth.

Outside, the colleagues and their partners called goodnights in civilised voices and got into their civilised cars.

"We'll need to drive home separately," Lucy said.

"*I'll* need to get a cab and pick up the motor tomorrow," Ed muttered. "Are you sure you can drive?"

"I didn't drink much," she replied.

He put his arm around her. "Come on – we'll all get a cab together. Then come down tomorrow. Together."

All during the drive home, Lucy could feel the moment coming: the one where she would tell Ed what the night had felt like inside her bones, where she would give words to the theft, she couldn't politely name. When they were in bed, she finally made her move.

"It was nice," Ed said, beating her to it, relief loosening his jaw. "Did you see how well Josie got on with them? She's a natural."

Lucy closed her mouth. "Yes," she said. "She is."

She tried again a minute later. "When she told my story—"

Ed stopped mid yawn and looked down at her. *Or is that what one might call a "scowl"?* "She didn't mean anything by it."

"Didn't she?" Lucy snapped.

"I think my little angel might be being a *tiny* bit sensitive."

"I am sensitive," Lucy said. "It was mine."

"It was sweet," he said. "It was all fine."

"Fine." Lucy moved uncomfortably in their silk sheets.

"She was good tonight, Luce. Don't you think?"

"Oh, she's very good. At almost everything, it seems."

"Don't start," he said, gentle, warning, tired. "Please."

"I'm not starting. I'm noticing." She rolled over and closed her eyes, knowing sleep would be a long way off.

Later, Ed began to snore, Lucy lay awake and replayed the evening: the way the table bent toward Josephine's voice, the way Ed's laughter rose above all others, the way her own words had sounded when someone else wielded them. She thought of the green dress dappling Josephine's body. She thought of Josephine before the mirror, painting Lucy's mouth onto her own face.

She understood then that copying wasn't the point. Copying was the wrapper. The sweet inside was something else. The trick wasn't to be Lucy. The trick was to be a better version.

As sleep finally came, Lucy asked herself some ugly questions. Had Ed noticed that Josephine was wearing her dress and said nothing? Did he care? Was he already slipping through her fingers?

5

October 31st

When Lucy woke, for long beautiful moments, the house felt ordinary again, obedient, as if a night's sleep could smooth the day before into nothing. Lucy reached for her phone where it always lived – edge of the bedside table, screen down – and found nothing.

Her hand met wood, but the edge was not where it should be. The table had shifted – an inch, maybe two – so the lamp's cord pulled strangely, so the glass of water sat just off its ring, a wet kiss stamped on the wrong grain. Definitely no phone.

Worse, her diary was not there either. She leapt out of bed. It was not on the floor, nor fallen between table and bed as it sometimes did.

She gripped her hair and tugged on it, something she thought people only did in books. Ed stirred.

"Did you move my table?" she asked, too anxious for morning.

He woke with a somehow annoyed yawn. "What?"

"My table. It's... wrong." She heard herself and wanted to edit the sentence. "Different."

He propped himself on one elbow and looked as if indulging a mad fantasy. "Looks fine to me."

"It isn't." She leaned over the side, peered into the narrow shadow where dust bunnies keep their secret congress. "And my diary's gone."

"You had it last night?"

"Yes. I wrote—" She stopped. She did not list what she had written after an hour of non-rest. Her demons were supposed to be private. Ed had never read her diary. "It was here."

Ed narrowed his eyes. "I didn't touch anything. You know tidying's not my thing."

"You tidied the other day," she said, trying to make light of it. "You even moved my shoes into the wardrobe. You're on a roll."

His mouth softened; his eyebrows lifted. "I moved one pair so we wouldn't both break our necks, Luce. I didn't mess with your bedside table." He sank back, put an arm over his eyes. "Maybe you left the diary downstairs."

"I didn't."

"Maybe you left it downstairs," he repeated, the way you say to a seven-year-old: *are you quite sure your coat isn't on the peg where coats live?*

She bit down on the answer she wanted to give and climbed out of bed. The floor was cold. Her bones were colder. The room smelled sleep-sour, the shadow of her perfume clinging to the sheets.

She checked the chair where yesterday's dress had slumped; the dressing table drawers, the foot of the bed, though she couldn't think why it would be in any of this place. As expected... nothing. Her pulse had found a tight, irregular beat that made her feel foolish.

"I didn't move anything," Ed said. "Honest."

"I heard the door," she said. "Last night. Once." She'd woken briefly to the small, soft sound of a hinge murmuring to itself. She'd counted to twenty, then sleep had taken her back with whispered promises it had been part of a dream. Not another part of this oh-so civilised nightmare.

Ed lifted his arm, looked at her as if she were written in a language that he couldn't read. "Josie's on the other side of the house," he said. "She wouldn't come in here."

Lucy didn't say: *she wore my dress*. Though perhaps she should have. But also, her bloody husband should've noticed. She said, "She might, if she needed something. A charger. Painkillers."

"She'd ask."

"She doesn't always," Lucy said, light, because if she said it any other way it would sound like an accusation.

He sighed and sat up, rubbed his hands over his face. "Do you want me to ask her?"

"No," Lucy said quickly. The idea of Edward knocking on his sister's door and saying, "Did you borrow my wife's diary?" made her throat burn. She added defiantly, "I'll find it."

She dressed quickly, uncomfortable in her own skin, her own house. In the kitchen the diary did not lie on the table beside the fruit bowl, where she sometimes left it after a burst of introspection struck her while preparing a meal or grabbing a snack. It was not by the kettle.

She moved to the living room. It was not on the sofa, under a cushion, by the TV. She could feel her schedule pleading for her attention: the journey to work; the lesson plans; the child whose aspirations didn't care if some strange creature was bullying her in her own home.

When Ed came down, hair damp, tie loose, he kissed the top of her head. "It'll turn up," he said, and because he wanted that to be a kindness she tried to let it be one.

After he left, the house held that hollow feeling Lucy normally didn't like. That *I'm home alone* feeling. She wasn't though. She felt like she never would be again. Was that overly dramatic?

She stood in the hall and felt the draft pulling the front door an inch, felt the faint vibration of the boiler deciding to work, felt the narrowing of a choice: say nothing, do nothing; or act, and act decisively.

She climbed the stairs. On the landing, the spare room door, once their room, stood ajar. She paused. Josephine's door, no, *her* door, was half open with the tone of an invitation.

Lucy knocked. "Jo?" Silence. She knocked again, a little louder, and pushed.

The room was neat in a way that felt performative. Their old guest bed, bought from a woman on a Facebook group who had advertised it as 'good as new' and meant 'survived a marriage we won't speak about', was made with military precision. Josephine's small suitcase lived at the foot, open like a stage set: a row of folded tops, underwear arranged by colour, a pair of designer jeans. On the dressing table, her toiletry bag sat with its mouth partly unzipped, showing the bone-white edges of sealed packets and black-handled brushes like scalpels.

Lucy moved to the table, then stopped, then moved again. She did not touch the zips. She did not open drawers. She looked, because looking is not a crime, especially not in one's own home: a book face down (not the kind Lucy read), an ankle chain, a receipt in Spanish for coffee and something else she couldn't translate. She turned to leave, then a smell struck her.

Am I bloodhound now?

It was there. She couldn't ignore it.

It was faint, not the heavy pulse of a sprayed wrist, but the ghost of her own perfume, the one she wore sparingly because it felt like a luxury you should keep only for special occasions.

Lucy stood very still. Smells travel. Perhaps last night she'd hung her cardigan on the banister and Josephine, passing, had touched it by accident. Perhaps the house itself had become permeable, and all their atoms were happily mixing and nothing meant anything at all.

Downstairs, her phone showed a text: *Love you, don't worry X.* From Edward, which meant he was worried. She typed back: *Found it. See you later X.* It wasn't exactly a lie because she *would* find it. The diary would reappear, abashed, its pages apologetic.

At school she couldn't stop thinking about the dress and the diary and the casual way her husband dismissed her concerns. One of the children asked why people wore masks on Halloween and Lucy snapped, "Wearing a mask is easier sometimes." The boys and girls exchanged looks.

Is Miss okay? she imagined them thinking.

The house was quiet when she got back. On the hall table, the post lay like bad news she wanted nothing to do with. Pessimism was corroding her from the inside.

Upstairs, the spare room door stood exactly as it had in the morning. In their bedroom, the bedside table had not moved back of its own accord. The diary had not crawled home. She washed her hands three times longer than necessary and watched the water do nothing but go away.

They hadn't meant to make Halloween a big thing. Children would knock; they'd hand out individually wrapped fun-size assurances to small vampires and slightly shy skeletons and the toddler dressed as a pumpkin who would cry when the mask made his nose itch. Ed had once carved a passable cat face into a pumpkin and declared the tradition complete. This year Lucy set the bowl by the door and found the good humour she kept for other people's children.

By eight, the street's chaos had thinned to occasional footsteps and a laugh that ran off before anyone could scold it. Ed dozed on the sofa like a man who had worked and eaten and earned his right to close his eyes in his own house. She liked when he slept like that, with a quality she couldn't quite put her finger on. *There's something primal and manly about it.* The TV played about emperors and engineering, narrator purring, pictures marching through a world that had already been made.

Lucy sat with her feet tucked under her, a cushion warm under her elbow, and allowed herself the small, precious trick of imagining that Josephine had decided to spend the evening with her parents. The doorbell rang. Lucy stood, glanced at Ed (still asleep, the smallest thread of drool bright on his lower lip), and went to it.

Three witches, one vampire, a parent in a puffer who said "Say thank you" as if the children had just committed a crime. Lucy admired costumes, doled out chocolate, said "Happy Halloween!" as if the words were a spell that would keep the house safe from tricks. She closed the door and returned to the living room satisfied with the easiness of tried-and-tested roles.

I give the sweets. You eat the sweets. It was simple.

Josephine was in her place.

Not sitting exactly, but poured there, the way water finds the shape of a bowl. The TV channel had changed to something fast and glossy where beautiful people lied into cameras. Josephine had the throw of her knees. Lucy's throw. She had also claimed Ed's shoulder. He had stirred, the way men do when warmth arrives; his head had tilted, his eyelids had admitted light, but he had not moved away because sleeping people are can get away with anything, apparently, like moving closer to his sister but not his wife.

"What are you doing?" Lucy said, not shouting, but sharp enough that the air itself winced.

Josephine didn't flinch. She rose slowly, smoothing the throw with two serene hands. Her smile was a careful shape that could be read as apology by an audience determined to be generous. "You're so touchy," she said, voice sweet as a pear. "I just wanted to watch something... less boring."

She stepped aside an inch. "There's room enough for all three of us."

No bloody thank you! Lucy's hands had begun to tremble.

Ed blinked awake. "Hey," he murmured, rubbing his face. He looked from Lucy to Josephine and then to the television and laughed softly. "Did I miss the trick-or-treaters?"

"A few," Lucy said. She kept her eyes on him because if she looked at Josephine, she would not be able to arrange her face into anything remotely cordial. "You were asleep."

"Still am," he said, with a smirk and a yawn. "Everyone okay?"

"Perfect," Josephine said. She lifted the throw and laid it back on the sofa politely. "You were snoring, Eddy. I woke you to save our ears."

"And you changed the channel," Lucy said. "I didn't even know you were home."

"I came in, went upstairs, got changed, then came down. Quiet as a cat, that's what Mummy always used to say, right, Eddy?"

"Hmm." Ed looked awkwardly at Lucy.

Josephine's eyebrows lifted, amused. "I did change the channel," she said, as if the confession were adorable. "I like noise. The narrator man was making me sleepy."

"It was my programme," Lucy said. She heard the child in it and despised the child and had no better sentence available. In fact, Ed had chosen the programme before falling asleep. But she had planted her flag now.

Ed set his feet on the floor, palms pressed against his eyes, the way he did when he was stifling a mood or reaction. "We can watch whatever. It's Halloween. We could watch a film."

"We could," Josephine said, agreeable. She reclaimed the throw's edge, folded it in a way that seemed territorial. "Or I could go. I've taken up enough of your cosiness. I should have better judgement. This is a husband-and-wife thing, right?"

Right.

"Don't be daft," Ed said. "Stay."

What?

Lucy stood in the doorway breathing the smell of chocolate wrappers and the faint, almost citrusy thread of Josephine's shampoo. The room felt mismeasured, a carpet laid half an inch off, a picture hung fractionally skewed. She wanted to say: *this is our evening; this is my cushion; this is our quiet*. She wanted to say: *knock before you move things; ask before you sit where I do; don't chang ethe channel*. She wanted to say: *leave my bloody diary alone*.

Instead, she said, "I'll make tea."

It was Ed's face, she told herself, succumbing to cowardice. Ed needed this to work. He didn't want them to fight.

"Two sugars," Josephine called.

Lucy stood at the kettle. She lined up three mugs. She performed the small ceremony of steam and milk and stirred sweetness like a woman who knows that some rituals hold, as if making tea made this normal or acceptable. When she returned, Josephine had not retaken her spot exactly, but she sat close enough to Ed that their heat had made a small climate, and the programme spoke a colourful nonsense that only people addicted to phones care about.

Lucy placed a mug by each of them, then folded herself into

the armchair. She took her time seating herself, hoping Ed would argue, would ask Josephine to move.

"Did you have a good day, Luce?" Ed asked, like a peace offering.

"In the afternoon, we discussed maps. The importance of boundaries."

Could she be any clearer?

"Useful," Josephine said. "So many people don't know where they end."

"Some people don't even know where they start," Lucy said tightly.

The TV laughed for them.

Later, when the film they hadn't agreed on ended and Josephine said goodnight with the cheerfulness of a student leaving a seminar she'd dominated gently, Lucy turned off the TV and sat back into the silence. The room was dark except for the soft glow of the TV and the streetlamps shining through the windows.

"She's testing me," she said. The sentence came out like a guess spoken as truth to see if it fits.

Ed stretched, bone click, shoulder roll, the body of a man who soldiered on without thinking about how he did it. "She's being herself," he said. "You're taking it personally."

"It is personal," Lucy said, quieter. "It's inside my house."

"Our house," he said automatically.

"Yes," she said. "But it's still my space. It's supposed to be a... refuge."

He looked at her for a long moment then closed his eyes as if searching for a political answer. "She'll settle," he said. "It's new. It's... a phase."

"She moved things," she said finally, like a woman stepping into cold water one inch at a time. "My table. My diary."

"Oh, Luce. We've talked about this. Maybe you bumped the table. Like I said, I'm sure the diary will show up." He looked at her for long moments, then realised it wasn't good enough. "Okay. I'll ask her tomorrow to be careful. Happy?"

"No," Lucy said. "But it's a start."

Asking Josephine to be careful made no sense. It wasn't as though, if she had stolen the diary, she'd done it by accident.

They went up to bed, and the house made the same noises it always did: pipes, the structure sighing, the fox outside pleading its midnight case. Lucy stood for a moment with her hand on the diary-shaped space that wasn't on the table, as if her palm could conjure what her efforts had refused to return.

When she lay down, Ed turned toward her and found her hand under the duvet, the way he often did. She let him. His fingers were warm. *Because he was snuggled up next to his sister. She kept him warm.* She held him despite her resentment, because love is like a boundary too, a line you draw and draw and draw until it looks like a country you can live in.

In the spare room, a door clicked softly shut. The house settled. Somewhere, the diary existed. Somewhere, someone had opened it and knew Lucy better than she had any right to be known.

Lucy lay with her eyes open in the dark and thought of the morning, when she would move the table back precisely where it belonged, and place a glass exactly on its pale ring, and buy a new notebook with a spine that would remember who it belonged to.

She slept in small fitful stretches. Just before midnight, she woke after what had felt like a long time but had only been twenty minutes. On her bedside table, there was nothing. The diary did not reappear.

But Lucy's certainty did, stubborn as a weed: whatever

Josephine was doing, it wasn't random. Boundaries weren't accidents. They were maps. And tonight, in front of the TV and Lucy's husband, Josephine had crossed yet another line and smiled while she did it.

6

November 2nd

The house at night had its own language. Pipes whispered to each other in the walls, the boiler gave a low, occasional sigh, and the wind rattled at the windows as if testing them. Lucy had grown accustomed to it. Every house she'd ever lived in made noises once people slept, but tonight she woke with the strange certainty that what she'd heard wasn't the house.

It was a voice.

Ed's.

At first, she thought she'd dreamt it, some residual echo of the day's arguments. But then she heard it again: low, deliberate, too measured to belong to someone muttering in his sleep.

She checked the clock: 12:37. Too late for him to still be downstairs, unless work had dragged him into some brief-writing spiral. But his voice was different. Softer. Secretive.

Sliding out from beneath the duvet, she moved carefully, each step rehearsed. She avoided the board by the wardrobe, the one that always betrayed her with a long, splintery creak, and padded across the landing and down the stairs.

A thread of yellow light stretched beneath the kitchen door. It shouldn't have been enough to set her heart racing, but there was something unnatural about it, about the fact that her husband was still awake, talking in the small hours, not to her. She pressed herself against the cool plaster of the wall, heart in her mouth.

"...she's doing better," Ed was saying. His voice was low, pitched differently than the warmth he used with Lucy... and now with Josephine, she reflected bitterly. Urgent. Tired. "Yes... it's different this time."

A pause.

"Yes, Mum," Edward continued, voice rougher now. "I know. But Lucy doesn't need to know everything."

Lucy's pulse hammered. Her name landed like a stone thrown into water, the ripples expanding until they shook her whole body. A sheen of sweat sprung up to cover every inch of her skin.

She shifted her foot, too quickly, and a floorboard gave the smallest groan. She froze, lungs burning, listening.

Edward sighed, heavily enough for Lucy to picture him pinching the bridge of his nose. "I'll handle it. Just... please, don't start with her. We need peace right now."

Peace. The word snagged. What kind of war were they holding at bay?

Silence, then the soft scrape of a chair. The phone clicked against the counter.

Lucy retreated fast, heart thundering, padded back up the stairs and slid beneath the duvet, arranging herself on her side, feigning the deep looseness of sleep.

It was instinct that drew me out of bed, she thought madly. *He was so quiet, but I heard him. Somehow. Because I know something. It's not just Josephine out to get me. It's Ed too.*

She pushed that vicious, ugly thought as far away as she could possibly get it.

The pillow smelled faintly of detergent; she concentrated on it, forcing her breath into a rhythm that didn't seem panicked.

Moments later Ed entered, his movements careful. He undressed quietly, slid into bed beside her, and let his arm rest over her waist. His breathing was quick, uneven, then slowed into something more controlled.

Lucy lay with her eyes open to the dark. She understood only one thing: everyone knew something about Josephine, something that made Ed and Susan speak in codes, in half-promises, in whispered confidences. Everyone but her.

And Ed had just confirmed what she had begun to suspect: he meant to keep it that way.

The next morning, the kitchen smelled of burnt toast and coffee. Outside, November pressed grey against the windows, raindrops sliding down the glass like the tears Lucy refused to cry for herself. Lucy sat at the table, her palms flat against the grain, forcing herself to wait for the right moment. The diary still hadn't reappeared. Her nerves still twitched from the night before, stretched tight as wire.

Ed stood by the counter, buttering his toast with quick, distracted strokes. The crusts scattered across the surface like careless confetti. He looked pale, as though he hadn't slept after all.

"Ed," she said finally. His name felt heavy, weighted with the question coiled inside it.

He didn't look up. "Mmm?"

"What aren't you telling me about Josephine?"

The knife paused mid-air. Butter gleamed on its edge. His shoulders stiffened but he didn't turn.

"Don't start the day like this, Luce." His tone was even, but the warning in it was unmistakable.

"I heard you." She kept her voice level, though her pulse skittered against her ribs. "Last night. On the phone with your mother. You said she's doing better. That it's different this time. That I don't need to know everything."

His face had set itself into that lawyer's neutrality, the one he used in court when he wanted to reveal nothing. "You were listening?"

"I was awake." Her voice cracked, but she forced it steady again.

He placed the knife down with deliberate calm, the scrape loud in the quiet kitchen. "It's private family business. That's all."

Private. The word was a wall, tall and impenetrable, and she was being told she wasn't allowed through.

Before she could reply, the door opened. Josephine drifted in, hair brushed sleek, dressed in one of her immaculate blouses as if she were about to step onto a stage. Her perfume, Lucy's perfume faint but familiar, trailed into the room ahead of her. She carried two Costa takeaway cups.

She placed one in front of Lucy, the other before Edward, her smile gentle and precise.

"Coffee," she said. "Strong. Just how you both like it. I thought we could start the morning with a special treat. *My* treat." Her tone was warm, conspiratorial, as though she were sharing a secret with them. She looked Lucy directly in the eye. "What would you like to know, then?"

The air seemed to thicken.

Edward's head snapped toward Josephine, a sharp warning

in his gaze. "Leave it," he said. The edge in his voice made Lucy flinch.

Josephine tilted her head, the smile never slipping. "Only trying to help. I couldn't help but overhear."

Maybe that was right. Maybe Josephine had no control over her actions, driven by some sick instinct. Lucy just wished her husband had warned her beforehand. Or cared enough to do something about it.

Lucy's throat closed. She stared at the steam rising from her cup and felt the trap close with it, the circle tightening around her: Josephine smiling, Ed loyal, Susan whispering on the phone.

Her husband had silenced her in front of his sister.

It wasn't just that Josephine was in their house. It was that Ed had chosen his side and he'd chosen it long before Lucy even realised the fight had begun.

7

November 5th

The rain had finally broken, leaving the streets rinsed and shining, the gutters slick with leaves. On Saturday mornings the town was always alive: families darting between shops, teenagers clustering outside the bakery for hot sausage rolls, mothers corralling prams into tight gaps. Lucy kept her coat buttoned and her scarf wound close, the damp still clinging to her hair. The café was already busy, windows steamed, chatter fogging the air. She pushed open the door and stepped into the warmth, scanning for the familiar figure at the corner table.

Charlotte waved, half-standing to catch her eye. She looked exactly as she always did: light brown hair scooped into a messy knot that managed to look stylish rather than careless, cardigan slung over a black top, a ring of coffee already bleeding into the edge of her notebook. She grinned when Lucy reached her.

"Finally," Charlotte said. "I was beginning to think you'd been swallowed by domestic bliss."

Lucy tried to smile but knew it didn't reach her eyes. "Something like that."

They hugged briefly, and Lucy slid into the seat opposite. The café was thick with the smell of roasted beans and warm pastries; children squealed from the play corner; cups clattered against saucers with the rhythmic precision of a soundtrack. It should have been comforting. It should have been ordinary.

Instead, Lucy felt the nerves vibrating in her body like a low electric buzz.

Charlotte noticed. She always noticed. "All right, then," she said, leaning forward, lowering her voice against the background noise. "What's going on? Your texts have been monosyllabic, Luce, which is always a warning sign. And you look like you haven't slept. Talk."

Lucy breathed out. The relief of being asked surprised her. Words crowded behind her teeth, jostling to be free. She wrapped her hands around the coffee cup, anchoring herself to its warmth, and began.

"It's Josephine."

Charlotte's brow furrowed. "Ed's sister? The mysterious one who missed your wedding?"

"Yep. She turned up."

Charlotte blinked. "Turned up... how?" She laughed awkwardly. "You make it sound like a magic trick."

I wish I could snap my fingers and make the bitch disappear.

"Just... walked in." Lucy gave a helpless little laugh, but it came out brittle. "As if she'd been invited. Only I hadn't been told."

Charlotte's mouth set in a line. "And she's staying?"

Lucy nodded. "With us. For now. Ed says it's temporary, but —" She shook her head, words tumbling faster. "It doesn't feel temporary. She's in everything. Acting like a domestic goddess in the kitchen, stealing my spot on the sofa, wearing my clothes, my perfume."

"Hold on. *What?*"

Lucy nodded. "I found her in one of my dresses the other day, trying on my lipstick. She cooked Ed's favourite meal and he wolfed it down like he hadn't eaten properly since he'd met me. She..." Lucy faltered, chest tightening. "She moves things. My diary went missing. She smiles as if I should be grateful, as if she's doing me a favour by taking my place."

Charlotte stared at her, stunned. "Bloody hell."

"I sound paranoid."

"No," Charlotte said firmly. "You sound like a woman whose boundaries are being stomped all over. That's not paranoia, Lucy. It sounds like she's testing how far she can go."

The truth of it made Lucy's eyes sting. She pressed her thumb against the cup to steady herself.

Charlotte leaned closer, her voice dropping further. "She sounds... obsessive."

The word slid into Lucy's ears like a diagnosis. She shivered. "Edward thinks I'm overreacting. He tells me to relax. But then I overheard him on the phone to his mother. Late at night. He said she's doing better this time. Different this time. And that I don't need to know everything."

Charlotte's eyes widened. "He said that?"

Lucy nodded, throat thick. "They're hiding something. About her. Everyone knows but me."

For a long moment Charlotte said nothing, just watched her with that clear-eyed, unsentimental calmness that had always been her superpower. Then she spoke slowly. "You need to be careful. People like that – they blur lines until you can't see where you end and they begin. Start writing things down. A record. Every time she crosses a boundary, note it. Otherwise, she'll make you doubt your own memory."

Lucy gave a quick laugh, embarrassed. "Like a detective with a case file?"

Charlotte didn't laugh back. "Like a woman protecting herself."

Lucy looked down at her hands. The idea of keeping a record felt both ridiculous and absolutely necessary. Proof. Anchors in the fog. "I don't want to seem... dramatic."

Charlotte softened then, reached across and squeezed her hand. "It's not dramatic. It's sane. And you're not imagining this. I believe you."

The relief that washed through Lucy was unexpected, hot, almost dizzying. To be believed. She blinked fast, hiding the tears that threatened.

"Thank you," she whispered.

They talked a little longer, about school, about Charlotte's latest disastrous date, about ordinary things that barely touched the edges of Lucy's storm. But even as she listened, Lucy felt steadier. Someone else knew now. Someone outside the Keaton circle. She wasn't entirely alone.

~

The evening of November 5th encroached coldly with a preview of winter. As Lucy turned the key in the front door, she thought of the last few days, Ed busy with work, Josephine hiding in her room, and Lucy doing nothing but thinking about what she was going to do, the action she was going to take.

The house greeted her with warmth and the smell of onions softening in butter. For one foolish second, she let herself imagine Ed had come home early, that he'd remembered she loved when he made dinner for her, that he'd wanted to surprise her.

But when she stepped into the kitchen, it was Josephine at the hob.

Who else? Lucy gritted her teeth.

Oh-so perfect *Josie.* Sleeves rolled up. Fiery red hair twisted into a knot. Movements assured, practised. A second pan simmered with steam, and the counter was strewn with groceries Lucy hadn't bought.

"You're back," Josephine said brightly, as if Lucy had been gone a week instead of hours. She stirred the pan, the spoon clinking softly. "I thought I'd make dinner again. Edward's favourite... again."

Lucy stood very still. "You don't need to cook."

"I want to." Josephine's smile was serene, unbothered. "Besides, you must be tired after school. Sit down. Let me help."

She ladled food onto three plates, moving with the ease of someone who already knew the cupboards, the cutlery drawer, the very shape of the room. Then she carried the first plate to the table, placed it at Ed's usual spot, and set the second deliberately in front of Lucy's chair.

Then Josephine pulled out Lucy's chair, not to offer it, but to take it. She lowered herself gracefully into it, smoothing her blouse as she settled, and positioned herself opposite Ed's seat.

Lucy's chest twisted.

The scrape of the chair's legs on tile was louder than it should have been. She forced a smile, lowering herself into the spare chair at the side of the table. The food smelled rich, comforting. It might have been delicious. She knew she wasn't going to taste a thing.

Ed came in moments later, loosening his tie, smiling faintly at the sight of dinner waiting. No briefcase. No folder full of case notes like he often had. Plus, Lucy hadn't heard the front door.

"Were you home before me?" Lucy asked, shocked.

"I've been home for an hour. A rare light day for me."

"Oh," Lucy muttered.

When Ed finished early, he often swung by the school to

surprise her. Or, at least, he had in the early days. It had only been months. Were they out of the *early days* already?

"This looks amazing," he said, dropping a kiss onto Josephine's head before sliding into his seat.

Lucy caught her breath. The casual intimacy of it – the ease of the gesture – stabbed sharper than it should have, considering what she'd witnessed so far. She folded her hands in her lap and told herself not to flinch. *Remember what Charlotte said. You're not mental, Luce. They are.*

No, she reflected quickly. *Josephine* was. Not Lucy's Ed. Right?

The three of them ate without conversation for long minutes. Knives clicked. Forks scraped. The radio played faintly in the background, cheerful nonsense that didn't belong in the thick air.

Lucy broke first. She forced her voice into politeness. "So, Josephine. You never told me much about your job abroad. What exactly did you do?"

Josephine looked up slowly. "You seem very, very curious about this."

"Isn't that natural?" Lucy snapped.

"Luce," Ed muttered, but Lucy ignored him.

"I did different things," Josephine said airily. "Nothing important."

"How long were you away?" Lucy pressed. "You must've been doing something important. Or interesting. Or... something, to be away from home."

Josephine shrugged lightly, spearing a piece of potato. "Years. Time blurs when you're moving. Barcelona, Paris, a little in Lisbon." She giggled with weird childish energy. "I floated here and there."

"And how long do you plan to stay?" Lucy made the question firm. It was time she stopped letting them bat her around like a tennis ball. Then she ruined it. "I'm sorry to be so blunt, but I think this question is natural too."

For the first time, Josephine's eyes flicked to Ed before answering. He shifted uncomfortably, pushing food around his plate.

"Oh, I don't know," Josephine said finally, her voice airy. "As long as it feels right."

Lucy caught the evasiveness, the deliberate refusal to pin anything down. The same pattern, again and again. She wanted to demand clarity, to say: *I live here, I have a right to know.* But Edward's silence pressed at her like a hand. She swallowed the words with her wine.

Josephine leaned back, dabbed her mouth with a napkin, and glanced toward the window where the night had gathered. "Are you planning to watch the fireworks tonight?" she asked lightly.

The question was ordinary, but it landed like a stone in Lucy's stomach. The mask Josephine wore was faintly mocking, and for a moment Lucy felt the world tilt, imagined Ed and Lucy laughing behind her back, joking about how far they could push her.

"Yes," Lucy said finally, absurdly proud of how steady her voice was. "We might."

Josephine smirked, as if that had been the right answer to a question Lucy hadn't known she was answering. Everything she did seemed to have an ulterior motive. It was exhausting.

The room held its silence. Somewhere in the distance, the first firework split the sky.

Lucy forced another smile, but inside her chest something twisted tighter still, a coil wound sharp.

Charlotte had been dead right: people like Josephine blur lines until you forget where you end and they begin.

And tonight, with Ed complicit in his silence, Lucy felt the lines fading fast.

8

November 8th

By the time the house exhaled its evening noises and the street settled into the kind of quiet that belongs to foxes and insomniacs, Lucy had rehearsed so many times it had begun to feel like a lie. She lay on her side, eyes open, counting the small familiar cues: the radiator ticking as it cooled, the neighbour's gate complaining, the soft creak of Ed turning a page beside her. He'd brought a brief to bed, which meant he wouldn't notice the heavy, frantic way she breathed.

"I'm going to get some water," she said.

"Mm," he said, not looking up. "Get me one too please, angel?"

Angel, he called her. But it felt fake. She was partly relieved and partly resented him for not catching her mood.

She took his glass, her glass, and moved through the dark like an intruder. She placed the glasses on the landing floor and stood for a second with her hands braced on the banister, the black square of the window reflecting a pale, resolute outline back at her. Downstairs, she could hear the TV. Josephine was still awake or, even better, perhaps she'd fallen asleep in front of the TV.

Then she turned without the water, padded across the hall toward the spare room.

The landing held its breath. At the far end, the spare room door, now Josephine's door, was pulled almost, not quite, closed. The kind of *almost* that asks to be corrected. Lucy listened for the usual giveaway noises; music on low, the rustle of a person moving in a room but heard only the house. She edged closer and pressed her ear to the door. Silence.

She could have turned back. She could have chosen the small mercy of not knowing, of letting boundary violations remain as paranoia and rage rather than proof. Instead, she palmed the handle and eased the door inward, flinching at imaginary hinges. It opened without a sound.

The room had that hotel tidiness Josephine cultivated, a bed made as if an inspector might arrive any second, corners sharp, the coverlet smooth enough to skate on. The dressing table was a still life: hairbrush aligned with perfume, the small velvet pouch that held Josephine's earring backs cinched closed with care. The suitcase was at the foot of the bed, unzipped a third of the way, as if interrupted: the same neat stacks of tops and underwear, a paperback facedown so that its spine bent like something apologising.

Lucy stood very still and tried to be a camera rather than a body. She wasn't here to rummage. She wasn't here to claim. She was here to find the thing that would force sense back into her life, that would prove she wasn't mad.

The faintest trace of her own perfume moved under the air. She ignored it and crouched by the bed, pressing her palm flat against the floorboards to steady herself and to feel, absurdly, whether the house might tell her which way to look. The gap between bedframe and suitcase showed less dust here, as if someone had taken a cloth to the area. She slid the suitcase toward her a hand's breadth and looked without touching: no diary. Of course not. She hadn't expected it. She expected nothing and everything.

At the dressing table she ran her fingertip an inch above the velvet pouch and stopped. She bent, peered at the mirror. There, at the edge of the frame, a tiny smear of foundation, a thumbprint, smudged and then half-polished away. Not evidence, only prophecy: a person who leaves marks and then makes them disappear.

Her eyes went to the top drawer. She waited long enough to hear her own breath, then eased it open on its runners. Inside lay order: spare tights rolled like ammunition, a glasses case, clipped receipts. She lifted the glasses case and felt a thin rectangle beneath. Not her diary. She already knew the dimensions of her book the way you know the shape of your own palm in the dark. This was a passport-sized notebook, black, neat, the cover blank. She did not open it. She respected the boundary, even as that thought made her jaw ache, and put everything back exactly as it had been and slid the drawer closed until it kissed the frame.

She turned to leave, already rehearsing her reason for taking so long. She'd tell Ed she'd gone to the toilet before getting their glasses of water.

Then the house betrayed her. The floorboard by the dresser sighed under her weight with a long, expressive wail, a sound she'd have sworn was not a floorboard but a small, outraged animal.

She winced. Downstairs, something shifted, the scrape of a chair, a pause, the energy of attention redirecting itself. Was she imagining that? She took one step toward the door, then another.

"Lucy?"

Ed's voice, too close. The landing light clicked on, washing the threshold in domestic yellow.

He stood in the gap, barefoot, shirtless the brief tucked under his arm. For one second, he simply looked confused. Then comprehension rearranged his face into something harder.

"What are you doing?"

The question was too large to answer truthfully. Lucy chose a sliver of it. "Looking."

"For what?"

"My things," she said, and felt ridiculous as soon as the words were out. "My diary. It's still missing. I looked everywhere. Someone must've taken it."

"Someone?" His tone transformed the word into a dare. "Or perhaps you misplaced it? Perhaps what you're doing here, Luce, is very wrong."

She swallowed. The shame of being unreasonable and the fury of being made to feel unreasonable burned through her. "I didn't forget."

Josephine's face appeared over Ed's shoulder, composed and pale. She wore pyjamas that looked more expensive than Lucy's good dress and a face scientifically calibrated to express pity.

"What's happening?" she asked, voice soft and innocent.

"Lucy was in your room," Ed said, not looking at Lucy now.

He sold her out. Just like that. No attempt to defend or explain.

Till death do us part, Ed. Have you bloody forgotten?

Josephine glanced at Lucy with a strange mixture of innocence and intimacy, as if this were a private misunderstanding they would laugh about one day. Then she stepped forward, hand to her chest. "You don't trust me," she said quietly, "in my own brother's house?"

Something in Lucy tilted. "It's my house too." She had meant for it to be calm but it came out raw. "And my things have gone missing. I'm trying to find them."

Josephine's face arranged itself into wounded grace. "If you'd asked, I would have helped you look."

"I've been asking." The words sounded dramatic even to her. She pulled them back and tried again. "My diary—" She stopped. "I just want my things where I leave them."

Edward's jaw worked, the muscle showing and disappearing as if trying to speak for him. "This is not okay," he said, carefully, the lawyer inserting himself between two people he loved.

But who does he love more? Lucy didn't want the answer.

"You can't go into her room, Luce. You can't search through her stuff."

"I didn't," Lucy said. "I looked. There's a difference."

"To you," he said. "Not to me. Not to her."

"Eddy." Josephine's voice touched his name and as if by reflex he turned, attention delivered like a gift. "It's fine. She's under stress."

"I'm under stress?" Lucy echoed, a laugh moving in her throat like a cough. "My things are missing."

"Your things," Ed muttered with disgust.

"Yes, my diary," she said, holding his eyes, willing him to remember who had bought it with her, how he had cradled her cheek and whispered it would help calm her overactive, beautiful mind down. "You know the one."

"It'll turn up," he said dismissively.

"I've looked," she said. "And other things. My perfume. My lipstick. My dress. My bloody dress! She,"

"She's my sister, Luce," he interrupted, and she realised with a kind of electric clarity that *sister* was an answer that absolved everything in the Keaton clan.

Josephine took a small step back, like a saint ceding the floor.

"I don't want to be a problem," she said gently. "I'll go. I'll book a hotel. I wouldn't want to ruin things between you."

She had no bag in her hand. Her hair, which she wore loose to sleep, fell perfectly, abundant and vivid red.

"No one is going to a hotel," Ed said, matter-of-fact. He turned to Lucy again, softer now, almost pleading. "This... this paranoia, Luce. It's... it's ruining everything. I'm trying to spend time with my sister. We've barely seen each other in years. Instead we have ninety minutes of peace then a fight."

Paranoia. The word handled her roughly, pushed her into a corner, tried to box her in.

"I'm not paranoid," she said, and hated how desperate her tone became. "I'm noticing. My dairy didn't just disappear. And she wore my—"

"Keatons don't pry," Ed said definitively. "And you're a Keaton now. We don't snoop either. If something's gone missing, we'll find it together, *in the morning*."

Josephine's hand touched his shoulder for a second, a benediction. "Leave it," she murmured, and Lucy felt suddenly sick. Leave it. Leave it. Was this how Keatons handled things, then? Ignore the problem and hope it went away. Or let Josephine do any damn thing she wanted without repercussions.

Lucy stepped into the hall, suddenly aware of her bare feet and the thinness of her T-shirt and the way night makes a stage out of banal details. The three of them paused in the little landing theatre, and Lucy wondered if she was the only one confused about her role.

Ed broke the silence first, moving past Lucy to the stairs. "Come on," he said, weary. "We're not doing this at midnight."

Josephine lingered just inside the doorway, her head tilted, her expression tender enough to bruise. "Goodnight, Lucy," she said, as if they had shared a delightful misunderstanding and would sort it in the morning with jam on toast.

Lucy walked into the bedroom ahead of Ed, cringed slightly when he shut the door behind her with a definitive click. He didn't slam it or anything like that, but he was in a dark mood. She knew that without even looking at him. She climbed into bed, retreated into the covers. He sat on his side with his back to her, shoulders rising and falling as he breathed hard.

"I need this time with her," he said simply. "I've missed her. I feel like I'm finally getting her back, and you're—" He exhaled and searched for words that wouldn't bruise. "You're making it difficult."

Or maybe he had wanted the words to bruise after all.

"I'm making it difficult," she repeated. Her hands began to shake. She curled them into fists and hid them under the covers.

"Please," he said. "Just try. For me. For a week. No searching rooms. No accusations. If something goes missing, we talk like normal people. Right now, every moment is fight or flight."

"She has been in our room," Lucy said quietly. "You don't need a courtroom to see it. You need eyes. Do you even care that she wore my dress?"

"I assumed she asked your permission," he muttered, climbing into the bed.

His tone told her otherwise. "You didn't even notice it was mine."

He lay on his back and closed his eyes. "I'm going to sleep," he said. "You can do the same, or you lie there thinking about lifting fingerprints off coasters. I can't do another evening like this."

"You're choosing her," Lucy said.

"I'm choosing quiet," he said. And then, devastatingly honest, "I'm choosing not to lose her again."

What about losing me? Lucy screamed in her mind.

"I'm getting a glass of water," she said, standing. "For myself."

Lucy left the bedroom, not looking at Josephine's door because the temptation to place her ear to it and was a humiliation she wanted with more urgency than made sense. She went downstairs and filled a glass of water, willing her hand to stop shaking.

Back in the bedroom, she closed the door and leaned against it until the cold came through her T-shirt. Ed lay on his side with his back to her, a polite line of space between his body and the edge. His breathing was heavy, either a man who was committed to pretending to sleep or who didn't care about his wife enough to stay awake and check if she was all right.

She moved through the dark to her side, to her table. She put the glass of water exactly in the ghost ring left by last night's glass and she sat on the end of the bed and stared at the little yellow notebook that wasn't there. There is an exhaustion that feels like a stain. Wash and wash and the shadow stays. She went to the wardrobe and took down the shoe box where she kept expired passports and other knickknacks. She didn't know what she wanted from it. Some sense of... her-ness? Lucy-ness. She put it back.

The mirror on the wardrobe door held her, pale and blurred in the low light. She stepped closer until she could see the small, unremarkable scars along her chin from teenage spots, and the way her mouth turned down when she wasn't managing it, and the shape of the doubt in her eyes.

Perhaps I did move the table; perhaps I did misplace the diary; perhaps I am, after all, making trouble.

She lifted her chin and shook her head. "No," she said, out loud, to herself.

Inside a drawer, hidden so it wouldn't be stolen, she knew, but she tried not to think of it like that, lay a second notebook: a newer one she'd bought for when she finished the old, same brand, different colour, still wrapped in the crisp paper. She slid the band off, opened the cover, and smelled the scent of blank pages.

Charlotte's voice returned clean and firm: Start writing things down. A record. Every time she crosses a boundary.

Lucy wrote the date at the top of the first page.

Then she wrote: *Diary missing. Perfume used without permission. Sofa—my place taken, twice. TV changed. Ed's shoulder. Kitchen—Josephine sits at my chair, serves me my plate. Phone call: "She's doing better... different this time... Lucy doesn't need to know everything."*

She added loudly, *SHE WORE MY BLOODY DRESS AND MY HUSBAND DIDN'T CARE OR NOTICE.*

She paused, the pen hovering. Her hand shook. She put the pen down and decided to check another drawer. Ed didn't stir. She wanted to chuck a bucket of water over him. Did he really not care about her?

She stood on his side of the room with his drawer open, knowing she wouldn't find the diary here, praying she wouldn't. She stood as if the act could summon an object into being. Then she went to the bookcase beside the window and began at the top.

Photo album. Travel guide with a boarding pass marking Rome. Old cookbooks with the recipes she pretended she'd make one day. Teaching manuals. A paperback she loathed and had refused to finish. At the far end of the second shelf, tucked as if it had sprouted there, sat her diary.

She stared at it, not moving, the way you watch a wild animal in your garden and hope not to make it bolt. She slid it free with two fingers, careful not to let the hard cover knock against the neighbouring spines.

It looked like itself, same coffee stain on the back, same pencil smudge that had always given it character. It looked like itself and yet her skin rose in gooseflesh, an instinct that says: *you are a stranger in your own home.*

She carried it to the bed and sat with it closed for a long time, the way you sit with a letter before deciding whether to read it. Then she opened to the last page she remembered writing and felt her heart move in her chest in a broken rhythm.

There were pages missing.

Not the rough, natural tearing of a person who has pulled a leaf and lost a corner. Two clean blocks, two places where the thread of the binding had been lifted with care, the leaves eased out, the little spines left naked. The edges were too neat. Whoever had done it had planned to take only what mattered.

Lucy placed her finger along the scar where paper had been and counted backwards. A week. Ten days. The entries missing were the ones she had written with the most heat: *We fought about the dress. She cooked his favourite meal. I'm ashamed by how much I care about my place on the sofa. The first night she slept in the spare room, and I lay awake listening to whether she stayed there.*

She flipped through, faster now, a sick speed. On another page, a second surgery: the meal at the gastropub, when Josephine had taken her clothes and her anecdote.

She closed the diary and held it against her chest. Her vision prickled. She stood and went to the mirror again and looked at herself, really looked, the way one looks at a suspect and asks whether suspicion is the cynical or the careful thing.

Her throat worked. "You did not imagine this," she said. Her voice was hoarse. "You did not."

She heard again Josephine's soft outrage in the hall: *You don't trust me in my own brother's house?* And Lucy understood, with a cold clarity that left her fingers numb, that the pronoun had been the point. Own. As in, what's yours is mine whether she liked it or not. As in, this is a game and oh-so sweet Josie was better at it than Lucy was.

She sank onto the bed and opened the new notebook again. Below the list she had begun, she wrote: *Found diary. Pages missing. Torn out neatly. The entries taken: my thoughts about her. The night she wore my dress. The pub. The sofa. The fear.* She wrote the words slowly, printing like a child to make it undeniable.

Then she turned to the old diary and, with the care of someone handling something broken, she slid the ribbon marker to the last intact page and closed it. She placed the book in the drawer beside the bed and locked it. She had never locked that drawer in her life. She had to go downstairs to fetch the little brass key from the bowl where they kept the detritus of life, and when she returned and turned it in the lock, the tiny click felt ceremonial.

Ed made a noise in his throat and rolled to his back. "Everything okay?" he asked, voice thick with the residue of sleep or the performance of it. *She's got me doubting if my husband is faking sleep or not. Jesus.*

"Yes," she lied. The truth: *No. But I will be.*

She turned the lamp off and slid under the duvet. The dark settled over her like a hand on fever. Somewhere in the house, a pipe knocked twice, as if signalling up to another conspirator in another wall. In the spare room at the far end of the landing, Lucy imagined the soft rustle of a person shifting, the whisper of pages turning, the slow, satisfied exhale of someone who got off on crawling into somebody else's mind.

She brought her hand to her chest and rested it over the place where the new notebook lay beneath the duvet, hidden but warm, a her hope, her weapon. She pictured Charlotte's face in the café, the certainty in it. *Start writing things down.*

"All right," Lucy whispered to the page she hadn't yet filled. "Watch me."

9

November 9th

The morning arrived grey and mean, a sky the colour of dishwater pressed low over the roofs. From the landing, Lucy could hear the house rehearsing its day: the kettle ticking toward a boil, the scrape of a chair, the radio turned down to an murmur as if the news might apologise for itself. She pulled on a cardigan and followed the smell of toast.

Edward was at the table already, shirt sleeves pushed to his elbows, scanning something on his phone stubbornly as if he didn't want to acknowledge the awkward war in his house. A plate waited in front of him, two triangles of toast, butter cooling to a sheen, hotel-quality fare. Beside the toaster, a single mug of coffee sent up its calm domestic steam.

Only one mug.

He glanced up when she came in. Noted her. Offered the pale smile you give a colleague when both of you are already late. "Morning."

"Morning." She put her bag on the chair back and, before

she could stop herself, she looked again at the place where her coffee should have been.

He saw the look. "Sorry," he said, too quickly. "I wasn't sure when you were up."

"I've been up," she said. She tried to make it light, a nothing. The nothings were accumulating.

He turned back to his phone, then set it down as if reminded by some internal solicitor of his marital obligations. "How'd you sleep?"

"Bits and pieces." She opened a cupboard, reached for a mug, purposefully clattered it against another and, even as she did this, noted how petty the rebellion was. "You?"

He shrugged.

You slept like a bloody log, Ed.

The toast snapped between his teeth. The radio muttered through a report about strikes on a railway line Lucy never used. She poured coffee and told herself it was not about a missed morning coffee; it was about being seen.

A moment later Josephine's voice arrived in the kitchen as if it was part of the 90s pop song that started to play. It was so loud and intrusive, Lucy thought she must've been coming downstairs. Then the shower hissed on. She was walking across the landing, but making her presence known as forcefully as she possibly could. Another salvo in the never-ending invasion.

Edward's eyes flicked upward and softened before he remembered to keep his face neutral. "She's up early."

"Apparently." Lucy stirred her coffee, clattering spoon against mug. *Click-click-click. Look at me like you look at her, Ed.* A sick thought. She buried it. The sound of Josephine singing threaded through the ceiling, tapping on Lucy's nerves. She placed the spoon deliberately on the saucer and made herself look at Ed instead of the ceiling. "Do you want anything for lunch?"

"I'll grab something," he said, already glancing back at his phone. "Long day."

"Mine too."

He nodded, but the nod landed nowhere. A quiet had moved in and unpacked itself between them, the kind that isn't comfortable because it knows its own name. She sipped the coffee that she had poured for herself, and it tasted fine and not like anything at all. The shower cut off. Josephine's warble continued as a satisfied hum.

Lucy glanced at the clock. If she left now she'd have time to photocopy the new handwriting sheets before the little ones descended. "I'm going," she said, too brisk.

"Have a good one," Ed said, clipped and short, as if she was just a mate.

She hesitated, wanting a hand on her arm, a joke, a look that said any of this aloud: *I see it. I see you.* Instead, the house offered her the sound of Josephine padding across the landing and the faint thud of a drawer. The decision made itself. Lucy took her keys from the bowl by the door, felt their familiar bite against her palm, and walked out without goodbye.

The cold had a wet edge that made everything metallic. Her car sat where it always sat under the maple, a rash of leaves bright against the windscreen like a temporary tattoo. She brushed them aside with the sleeve of her cardigan, unlocked the door, and slid in. For a minute she let the engine idle, the fan pushing out stale night. She looked at herself in the rear-view mirror, tired, competent, a woman who got on with it, and muttered, "Right."

The road out of their street was quiet except for the sound of early vans and one cyclist cutting angles like a man who held an unrealistic, zealot's belief in his own luck. Lucy drove on autopilot, the familiar rhythm soothing her. She turned the radio on low. The presenter said something breezy about fireworks and the cold snap, and she turned it off again, her thoughts loud enough on their own.

At the junction by the bakery, she pressed the brake to ease into the queue and felt... something. Not the usual smooth assent of the pedal, not the reliable slight give-and-hold. There was a softness, then a tiny, troubling shiver in the pressure, as if she'd stepped on a throat.

She pressed again, harder. The car obeyed, but a fraction late, the way children do when they're testing if you mean it. She frowned, feeling with her foot. Maybe it was the wet. The road was slick with night. Maybe the garage had overpromised on last month's service.

She pulled away, anxiety a low thrum beneath her ribs now, and tried the brake again at the next zebra crossing. Softness, compliance, then that shiver. She told herself it was nothing and adjusted her following distance like a woman preparing for someone else's mistake.

At a roundabout she signalled left, watched a father in a suit shepherd a child desperate for his attention across the road, smiled despite herself, and eased into the turn. A white van came up fast on her right, failed to indicate, surged past. She exhaled and focused on the road, but sweat had begun to slide down the back of her neck.

Josephine has made me paranoid, Lucy thought bitterly. *Everything and everyone is a threat.*

It happened all at once, but time also somehow slowed.

She approached the junction; the light ahead turned amber to red; she pressed the brake the way she had every morning since starting at this school. The pedal went down, but it offered less resistance than it should. A half second hesitation. The car did not stop in the old obedient way; it negotiated. The bonnet crossed the white line. A horn cut the morning. A small blue hatchback, which had been trying to catch the amber and clearly thought she'd been doing the same, swerved. Lucy yanked the wheel left, missed a bollard by a hair, felt the tyres judder over the pavement. Someone shouted from another car. Thank God, no pedestrians.

The light stayed red. Everything else kept moving.

She had stopped. She had not stopped. Late. Crooked. Heart going too loud, hands slick on the wheel. Her mouth tasted of metal. She waited for the punch of guilt or anger or something from the other drivers and found only the tail of the moment disappearing into the road ahead. Nobody got out. Nobody died. The blue hatchback corrected and carried on. The horn noise receded as if embarrassed.

She backed the car up to the red light, sitting very still, breathing the air of someone who was almost just involved in a fight-or-flight incident. Her head went bright, then dim. She placed her hand on the dashboard as if apologising to the car for speaking too sharply. "Okay," she said to the wheel. "Okay."

When the light changed, she signalled. She took the turn. She made the next three braking points with exaggerated care, like a parent teaching a toddler not to run in socks. The car stopped each time, but the wrongness was there, tiny and insistently real. Soft, then shiver. Not failure. A flinch.

At the staff car park, she pulled into her usual spot and sat through the closing seconds of the song on the radio as she tried to gather her nerves. When the silence came, she turned off the engine and listened to the cooling ticks of a machine deciding to rest. She should call the garage, she thought. She should call Ed and say, calmly, that something in the brakes was off. She should be a normal, practical person who noticed a thing and dealt with it.

She reached for her phone and saw the last message she'd sent to Charlotte: *I might come by later if that's okay.* The banal relief of that made her eyes sting. She put the phone down, locked the car, and went to coax thirty children into some semblance of order.

~

The classroom saved her for hours. There is no room in a teacher's morning for obsessive thoughts; there is only glue and pencils and the bottled lightning of bright and enthusiastic children. Lucy poured herself into registers and tectonic plates and simple maths problems. She watched two boys argue about who owned the blue crayon and negotiated a treaty. She kneeled to tie a shoelace and stood too fast and almost knocked herself out on the corner of a table and laughed, because laughing in front of them made them – and her – feel safe. She read the first page of a story about a wolf who wanted to be a poet and they laughed at the idea with unfeigned joy, and for a whole three minutes she forgot the way the brake had decided to hesitate.

The end of the day brought more quiet. More thoughts. The silence after the children were collected felt cavernous. In a way thought, she loved this emptiness, the flotsam of paper, the small stray sock, the chairs perched on tables like birds, the knowledge that the room would forgive the madness and be ready again tomorrow. The light through the high windows had gone thin and wary; rain threatened.

She sat at her desk and opened the new notebook. Date. Time. She wrote: *Car brakes soft and shivering. Junction by the park, near miss of a bollard, drove onto pavement.* Her hand steadied. Recording was a kind of prayer.

The phone buzzed beside the notebook. She glanced down, expecting Charlotte or a calendar reminder to drink water, and saw instead a notification from a number she didn't recognise: no name, no picture, local area code.

She opened it.

Accidents happen. Take care.

Just that. Four words. No indication of who it was or how they'd known she was almost in an accident. The words remained as if printed on her skin.

Cold ran over her scalp and down her arms, the way it does when you lose your footing on a step in the dark and, for a second, you are still falling. And, for a second, you think you'll never stop falling.

No one knew about the near miss. She had told no one. The classroom had been full of children who either didn't have phones or, if they did for some silly reason, didn't have her number. She hadn't called the garage. She hadn't called Ed. She had driven to work and mentioned the near crash to nobody, and now a stranger was telling her that accidents happened.

She swallowed and stared at the message.

It could be a wrong number. It could be a scam. It could be... what? Who would write that if they had no idea what had happened?

She typed: *Who is this?*

She didn't send it. She watched the question flash in the little blue bubble of possibility and then go dim. She could see every version of the reply: a shrug, a denial, a second message worse than the first. She thought of Josephine's soft voice in the hall last night – *You don't trust me in my own brother's house?* – and the way the sentence had demanded a screaming *yes* Lucy had been too afraid to give. She thought of the brakes, the way they had softened, the way the pedal had gone down the extra fraction, the size of doubt.

She wrote the number at the top of a new page in the notebook and underlined it twice as if that might give it meaning. Then she screenshotted the message (proof: time, date, the ugly words), archived the thread into a folder she titled Notes and silenced unknown senders for the rest of the day. It was the digital equivalent of placing a thing under a glass and labelling it: specimen, do not touch.

I should text them back. I should do something.

But Lucy was beginning to realise something about herself. She was very good at burying things. Probably too good.

Her body needed movement, activity. Too much restless energy. She stood, found herself stacking glue sticks into colour families for no sane reason, and put them down again. She went to the window and looked at the car park, at her car sitting familiar and wrong in its space. She pictured pressing the brake and finding nothing beneath it. She pictured the loop of the brake cable where it lived under the chassis, how a person might weaken a line without cutting it, how you might test a boundary without leaving fingerprints.

Don't be absurd, she told herself. *You're a teacher, not a detective. You don't know how cars work beyond the bits that touch your hands.*

But someone knew she hadn't stopped in time.

The rain began. It sifted down in a careful sheet that blurred the view into a watercolour. The houses beyond the playground became gentler, the edges of the day softened. Somewhere in the building a hoover worried at a carpet; a laugh bubbled from the corridor and then stifled itself. Lucy picked up her phone, thumbed to Charlotte's chat, and typed: *Are you in? I could really do with that cup of tea.*

The reply came almost at once, as if Charlotte had been looking at her phone for no good reason and now had one: *Always. Come. I have fancy hipster biscuits shaped like leaves and I am prepared to be judgy about you-know-who.*

Lucy smiled despite the iron under her ribs. She closed her laptop, put the notebook in the front pocket of her bag (not in the main compartment, not where Josephine might search first), and turned off the lamps. She walked down the corridor, the sound of her own footsteps seeming impossibly loud in a building that had held children hours ago and had not yet forgotten them. She normally found this sound reassuring. Not today.

Her phone was heavy in her pocket. The message text had taken on a new weight, as if each letter had been typed in metal.

Accidents happen. Take care.

She walked down the slope to the car park, where the rain made the asphalt glitter like scales. She climbed in, turned the key, listened to the engine come up like a friend who hadn't yet chosen a side. She put the car into gear and placed her foot on the brake experimentally. Soft. Then that tiny shiver again, like a whisper. She took her foot off and sat for a second, both hands at ten and two, a picture from a poster about safety.

"Okay," she said to the car. "I hear you."

She put the car into drive and rolled forward gently. But after the first brake, she knew it was madness going on like this. She rang Charlotte and put her on loudspeaker.

"I'm going to be a couple of hours later. I need to take my car to the garage then catch a taxi to yours."

"Is everything okay?" Charlotte asked.

Not even close. "We'll speak more when I get there."

"I'll order Thai food. We'll make a night of it."

"Are you sure you don't mind?"

"I'm looking forward to it."

She kept the speed low for the first half mile and used the brake the way you test the temperature of bathwater, careful, ready to pull back. It held. Each time it held. But the doubt remained. She reached the garage and, with a crazed determination that was unlike her, blurted, "I want you to put a rush on this. Check the brakes. I'll pay extra if you can get me a quick answer."

The mechanic tilted his head. "Could have a look today, depends on how keen you are."

Lucy said she was very keen. She was pay-stupid-prices keen. The mechanic was happy to hear that.

When the taxi turned onto Charlotte's Street, her shoulders dropped an inch. A little terraced house at the end wore its winter fairy lights early; a cat sat fatly on a radiator inside a bay window and watched her with lazy contempt.

She took her phone from her pocket, opened the unknown sender's message again, and looked at the four words until they lost meaning. She thought about sending them to Ed with a demand to know what it meant, as he if knew. What if he did? What if he was in on this, all of it?

She closed her eyes, took a breath, thought about the look he would give her, the one that said, *we're living in different versions of the same house.* She put the phone away.

"Are you all right, miss?" the taxi driver said.

Again, she thought, *Not even close.* "What do I owe you?" she asked.

Charlotte's door opened before she could knock, as if she had watched her arrive. "Get in," Charlotte said, pulling her into the warmth. "You're wet and I've lit a scented candle."

Lucy laughed, the sound escaping her like a breath she hadn't known she was holding. Behind her, the street glowed, the kind of November light that makes a person think of fireworks and hints at Christmas. She wiped her feet, stepped inside, and felt the thin armour of the day crack in the only safe place it still could.

10

November 10th

Charlotte's house smelled like soy, ginger, and the faint medicinal sweetness of a candle that claimed it was "forest after rain." Charlotte had her laptop open, charger snaked across the rug, tabs blooming along the top like a rash. Raindrops poured down the windows in neat, cold diagonals. Thai food sat on the coffee table of her living room.

"Start at the beginning," Charlotte said, tucking her feet beneath her and spearing a spring roll. "Not the polite version. The real version. And share some of this food with me, please. I ordered way too much... And I *will* wolf it all down myself."

Lucy exhaled. It took four sentences before her voice stopped shaking. She told Charlotte about the brakes and the message from the unknown number. She watched Charlotte's face, how anger and concern took turns; how disbelief never once broke through. That was the most important part. Charlotte believed her without hesitation.

"Okay," Charlotte said when Lucy fell silent. "We stop guessing and start checking."

"What do you mean?"

Charlotte took Lucy's hand. "Look at me, hon. Do you seriously believe Josephine could do this?" When Lucy hesitated, Charlotte snapped, "Lucy, if you think there's even a *small* chance she's behind this, we have to check."

"Check what?"

"Who the hell she is." She spun the laptop halfway toward Lucy. "Spell her name exactly."

"Josephine Keaton." The keys rattled. The results page loaded, harmless at first, LinkedIn ghosts, a school prize from 2005, an out-of-date family fun run where a girl who might have been Josephine smiled at the edge of the frame. Charlotte refined the search the way only someone who lived on the internet knew how to do, quotes, minus signs, a local paper's archives.

The headline was small, the kind of thing that wouldn't be of note unless you happened to be living with the subject: **Local Woman Jailed for Violent Assault**. A date. A byline. A photograph taken from too far away to be certain and close enough to be devastating.

Charlotte clicked.

The article wasn't long. It didn't need to be. Two paragraphs set the scene – restaurant, late, an argument that became a scene, a witness statement about shouting – then the single sentence that shattered everything: *The defendant, Josephine Keaton, 27, attacked her brother's girlfriend, striking her repeatedly with a glass bottle and causing severe lacerations and a concussion; the victim was hospitalised for over a week.* A line about "intent to cause grievous bodily harm," another about a plea that slid from denial to diminished responsibility, and then the judgement: *three years' imprisonment.*

There was a quote from the judge about control and anger; a quote from the victim's family about recovery; nothing from

Josephine. A final sentence: *Keaton had no fixed abode at the time of the incident.* Not abroad. Not Paris. Not Barcelona. Not floating between glamorous jobs.

Lucy read it once. Then again. Each pass carved a deeper groove in her. "'His girlfriend,'" she said, the words tasting like metal.

Charlotte steadied the laptop with two fingers as if the news might cause it to explode. "Previous," she said, gentle. "Before you. There's no saying she would do the same—"

"She attached his *girlfriend*. Who knows what she would do to his bloody wife!"

Lucy stared at the photograph. Grainy, yes. But the bone structure was there, the mouth set into a careful line, the posture confident even in defeat. The undeniable fiery red of her hair. Josephine had pleaded guilty. Josephine had gone to prison. Josephine had not been roaming elegantly abroad. She had been caged like the animal she was behind her civilised smile.

"My God," Lucy whispered, not sure whether it was a prayer or a curse. "He knew."

Charlotte didn't say *of course he did*. She had mercy. She said, "Yes, he knew. And that sucks. But at least *you* know now. For sure. Your instincts were right."

The phone chose that beat – perfect, theatrical – to buzz on the table. Lucy flinched. Unknown number, she thought, before she looked. But it was the garage.

She answered. "Hello? That was quick."

A man's voice, brisk, apologetic. "Mrs Keaton? Sorry for the late call, but you said it was urgent?"

"Yes. Very."

"We've had a look at the brakes."

Her whole body leaned toward the words. "Yes?"

"Pads are fine. Discs are fine. It's the fluid. You were low, very low. We flushed and refilled, but—" He hesitated, as if he was afraid of her reacton. "It's not wear and tear. It's fresh. Like it's been drained recently."

Lucy pressed her fingers into the arm of the sofa to stop them from shaking. "Drained? You mean... tampered with?"

A beat. "I can't say that, officially. But the cap was replaced wrong. Threaded. Not an accident you get from topping up at a petrol station."

"How—when—" Lucy could hear herself slipping into gasps. She let out a long breath and tried again. "Is it safe now?"

"It is," he said quickly. "We've sorted it. But keep an eye, yeah? And maybe park somewhere less... accessible. If you can."

She thanked him, hung up, stared at the wall until the paint blurred.

Charlotte's voice came from far away. "Brake fluid? Did I hear that right? I'm sure that's what he said."

"Drained." Lucy's voice didn't sound like hers.

Charlotte sat back, her mouth opening into an O of fury. "Jesus." She pushed the laptop aside and reached for Lucy's hands. "You're not imagining this. You're not paranoid. Someone is playing with your life."

They didn't say Josephine's name. They didn't need to.

Lucy took the phone and opened the unknown text again and slid it across the table. Charlotte glared, colour rising along her cheekbones. "We go to the police," she said. "Tonight."

"And tell them what? A message and a feeling? A cap threaded wrong?" Lucy wiped at her eyes with the heel of her hand. "They'll say it was a freak accident no matter what the mechanic said. They'll say nobody hurt me." She swallowed. "Yet."

Charlotte's jaw worked. "We report it, Luce. We have to... and we tell Edward everything. All of it. You know about the article, what she did. If she did that, then she's capable of the car. Make him choose with the truth in front of him."

Lucy pictured his face, how it closed into neutrality when he looked at her, how it lit up when he looked at his sister. She nodded anyway. "He's good at not choosing."

Charlotte stood, businesslike. "Then we make it so obvious he can't ignore you." She closed the laptop with a firm, satisfying click and reached for her shoes. "I'm coming with you."

Lucy shook her head. "Nuh-no. Thank you. I need to try first. If I don't... I don't know what we're even saving."

Charlotte didn't argue. She hugged Lucy hard, the kind of hug that gives spine. "Call me the second you want me," she said into Lucy's hair. "No silent suffering. I'll be there with biscuits and a crowbar."

Lucy almost laughed. Almost. "I know."

"First, finish off some of this food while I print that article for you."

Twenty minutes later, she stood, gathered the laptop printout Charlotte had made like a soldier tucking a dispatch into her coat, and felt the day tilt onto a new axis. She rushed across the street to the waiting taxi. As she climbed in, she thought about telling it to take her someplace, anyplace, that wasn't home.

~

The house looked ordinary from the street, sash windows catching the last of the light, the hallway lamp pooling gold on the floorboards. Inside, it smelled of bleach and rosemary, as if someone had cleaned the counters just hard enough to make the place look like itself. Ed was upstairs. She heard the murmur of water, the squeak of a tap, his familiar cough. Josephine was... nowhere, and everywhere.

Lucy went to the bedroom and set the news article printout

on the bedspread, paper a stark white against the dark blue duvet. The headline looked bolder here.

Ed came in towelling his hair, tie gone, comfortable and domestic and frustratingly handsome. "Hey," he said, voice cautious, as if the house had already told him something was off. "Good time at Charlotte's?"

She didn't answer. She gestured to the news article so there was no way he could ignore it.

He didn't take it. His eyes tracked the title, the photo, the block of text; his face changed with each line, not with shock, but with the recognition of a moment he'd delayed as long as he could. But still, he didn't take it.

She huffed and picked up the printout. "You forgot to mention this."

He sat on the edge of the bed and finally took the paper from her hand.

"It's true," he said, into the quiet.

Lucy's breath hitched. The simplicity of it was almost a kindness. "She attacked your girlfriend. She put her in hospital. She went to prison."

"She was... unwell." The word felt rehearsed. "She'd lost everything. It was... complicated."

"Complicated?" Lucy heard her own voice rise into a register she didn't like. She flattened it. "She savagely attacked a woman with a glass."

"She paid for it," he said softly. "She paid. She did the time. She came home and – God, Luce – she needs protecting, not punishing. Mum is... Mum keeps her on rails, and sometimes it works, and sometimes it doesn't, and I—" He broke off, helpless, and rubbed his hand over his face as if he could wipe away the past. "I was trying to give her a chance. With me. With us."

"With me," Lucy corrected. "Without telling me who she is."

He looked up quickly. "That's not who she is."

"It's part of who she is, Ed," Lucy said. "You can't deny that. You *can't*. That's the gaslighting Olympics, Ed, and you know it. This is part of her. And you hid it."

"I delayed it." He tone had become dark, almost argumentative. "I wanted you to know her first. Her humour. Her unique sense of... of Josie-ness. Not that one mistake. It's not fair for it to define her."

The line was beautiful and rotten. Lucy sat beside him, careful not to let their bodies touch. "Do you know what else I learned today? Someone drained my brake fluid." She watched the words slam into him. "The cap was threaded wrong. Not wear. Not age. Interference. I had the garage do a rush job after school. Because I suspected something, Ed. Do you understand what I'm saying here?"

He stared at her, then shook his head hard too hard, as if force could make reality into a different shame. "That's not... someone made a mistake. Or the mechanic's—"

"Accidents happen," Lucy said.

He blinked. "What?"

She shook her head. "Nothing." Somehow, the message seemed a step too far. He would just make more excuses. It was all he did when it came to precious Josephine.

"Luce, please." He reached for her hand; she left it in her lap. "You're looking at everything in the most pessimistic way. Where's my bright, happy teacher, huh?"

"You're refusing to see what's in front of you," she said, not biting on his loving tone.

"My sister is trying. Here. At home. To be part of our family." His voice broke on the word home, and for a second she saw the protective, loving little boy from all their childhood stories. She felt something that used to be love and discovered it was grief.

Footsteps in the hall. Lucy's shoulders locked. Josephine appeared in the doorway as if the scene had been called and she was making her entrance, fiery hair loose, makeup immaculate, a silk blouse that suggested she belonged wherever the hell she wanted to. She rushed across the room and snatched the paper from Edward's hands, then arranged her face into sympathy.

"Oh, Lucy," she said, the softest pity. "You've been watching too many trashy TV dramas."

"Get out," Lucy said, surprising herself with the speed of it.

Josephine leaned her shoulder against the doorframe instead. "Brake fluid," she went on, almost amused. "Mechanics love that one. It's the oldest trick in the book. Drain a bit, sell you an emergency. Your so-called expert is probably a cowboy squeezing you for cash. Don't be naïve."

The word naïve landed like a hand across the cheek. Lucy stood up so fast blood rushed to her head. "How did you—"

"Your voice carries," Josephine said. "Houses do that. They pass messages along. Didn't you know?" She smiled at Ed, almost tender. "We were just children when we learned that."

Ed didn't smile back. He had gone still, but he wasn't fighting, wasn't defending his wife. He looked so uncharacteristically weak. "Jo," he said quietly. "Not now."

"Not now," Josephine echoed, her tone one of pure disgust. She shifted her gaze back to Lucy. "I'm sorry you're upset. Truly. Maybe a hot bath? Some reality TV? Turn your brain off? It works wonders." The sympathy in it was so precise it seemed psychopathic.

Lucy forced herself to breathe. "You took my diary. And I think you messed with my brakes too. I don't care what you say."

Josephine blinked like an innocent child. "I can't believe you'd think that about me, sweet sister-in-law. If you think I'm capable of that, I have no idea how you're managing to get any sleep with me just next door..."

"Hear that, Ed?" Lucy snapped. "That was a threat, plain and simple."

"Oh, gosh." Josephine rolled her eyes. "A threat? Are you fuc—"

"Enough," Edward said, finally, the word carrying the weight he should have put into other sentences, days ago. "Jo, please."

Josephine didn't move for a long heartbeat. The atmosphere grew tenser. Then she gave Lucy a small nod as if conceding a point in a game Lucy hadn't understood she was playing, and stepped back into the hall. "Goodnight," she said softly, and vanished.

Quiet again. Only the tick of the bedroom clock and, far off, a firework unspooling and dissolving.

Lucy looked at Ed, her weak and once wonderful husband. "You knew," she said, but there was no accusation left in it. Only fact. "About the girlfriend. About prison. About who she was. You knew she might hurt me. You brought her here and you didn't tell me who was standing in my kitchen."

He put his hands on his knees and stared at the carpet as if he might disappear into it. "I knew," he said. "I made a bad choice, Luce."

The simplicity of it sliced her. She sat on the edge of the bed, felt the mattress dip and fail to catch her, and said, because there was no safe way to save anything now, "This is how marriages break."

He flinched. "Don't say that."

"Then don't make it true."

She could have shown him the message. She felt her hand twitch toward her pocket, the proof hot against her thigh. She could have turned the phone, so he saw the ugly words: *Accidents happen. Take care.* She imagined the two outcomes, both real: he believed the obvious fact it was Josephine; he made absurd excuses. She saw Josephine's face at the door and knew which way the coin would fall.

She left the phone where it was.

"I'm sleeping in the other room," she said, though she had nowhere to go that didn't make her feel exiled in her own house.

Ed stood, defeated. "Don't." He reached for her and stopped. "Please."

She stepped past him, out into the hall that had begun to feel like a corridor in a hotel where doors are only numbers and none of them belonged to her. The spare room door was closed, the tiny strip of light at the threshold a quiet insult. Lucy walked past it to the small room at the back. She shut the door with the gentleness of a person who has decided not to wake a sleeping child and leaned her forehead against the wood until the cool steadied her breathing.

Down the road, late fireworks finally began in earnest, shrieks, blooms, the sky cracking into flowers that died in seconds and left smoke. She closed her eyes and imagined the colours, so much brighter than this house, this life. The house absorbed the sound and gave it back small.

Lucy lay on the narrow bed and listened to the show she could not see.

"Accidents happen," she murmured, thinking of all the nasty things that could happen to Josephine. "Take bloody care."

11

November 11th

The rain had begun before dawn, slanting against the kitchen windows in sheets, blurring the garden into something waterlogged and anonymous. The light was thin, more November than morning, and the whole house carried that damp quiet of a weekend where nobody wanted to move.

Lucy stood by the counter, her hands braced on the cool wood. She had been waiting for him, listening to the creaks upstairs, the slow drag of his feet on the landing, the pause at the bathroom sink. She'd watched the second hand of the clock crawl around as she rehearsed her questions, the weight of the printout still fresh in her mind. She held an empty mug, but somehow, actually making the coffee felt like too much.

When Ed finally appeared, hair damp, sleeves rolled, she was ready.

"Why didn't you tell me?" Her voice came out steady, though she could feel her pulse hammering in her throat.

Ed frowned, reaching for the kettle as though he hadn't heard. "Tell you what?"

She almost threw her mug at him. "Ed."

He avoided her gaze. "I just got up."

"Don't say things like that anymore. *'Tell you what?'* It's insulting. You know what." She set the mug down too hard, the sound sharp against the silence. "Prison. Josephine's sentence. The assault. That article."

He stilled. For a moment the only sound was the rain tapping furiously against the panes. His shoulders twitched as if the words had grazed him, and then he sighed, dropping them low, as though she had asked him to carry too much.

"Lucy, that was years ago. Ancient history." He leaned against the wall, hands stuffed in his pockets. "Today's a new day."

"You can't just brush this under the rug."

"It's not your concern."

"Not my concern?" She laughed darkly, the sound brittle and too loud in the muted kitchen. "She's in my house. At my table. Wearing my clothes. Breathing down my neck. And you think her violence, her prison record, isn't my concern?"

Edward turned, jaw tightening. "I've told you, Luce. She's my sister. She made mistakes. She paid. You dig up old dirt, and for what? To punish her twice?"

Lucy stared at him, disbelief tightening every muscle. "No. To understand who I'm living with. Who you've invited in without telling me the truth."

His voice sharpened, rising above the rain's percussion. "If you loved me, you'd understand."

The words sliced through her like glass. *If* she loved him. As though love required blindness. As though loyalty meant silence.

Her chest ached with betrayal. "Don't you dare," she whispered. "Don't you dare tell me what love looks like when all you've done is lie."

The rain lashed harder, streaking the windows, thunder

muttering low in the distance. The kitchen light flickered, as if the house itself were uneasy with what it was hearing.

Ed's eyes darkened, his mouth working as if to form another defence, but his silence was worse than words. Lucy's hands clenched around the counter edge until her nails pressed crescents into the wood.

It was all there, plain: his loyalty bent not toward her but elsewhere, toward the woman upstairs.

And just as the air between them reached breaking point, the sound of soft footsteps carried down the stairs.

Josephine strolled into the kitchen as though she'd been waiting for the exact right moment in their argument, her entrance choreographed to perfection. Her hair was loosely tied, her face scrubbed clean, but around her shoulders hung one of Ed's sweaters, grey and soft, the sleeves too long, making her look both fragile and claimed.

This is worse than misplaced loyalty, Lucy thought as rage swirled through her. *This is goddamn incestuous loyalty.*

Lucy pushed that ugly notion away. That was too far. She needed to calm down. But Ed was driving her over the edge again and again until falling was her new norm.

That sweater was hers by marriage, by routine, the one Lucy had worn after the first time they'd had sex, sneaking to the bathroom in it, returning and seeing Ed look at her like she was perfect. And now it was draped over Josephine like a trophy.

Ed's entire body changed at the sight. His face softened, his jaw unclenched, the sharpness gone as if it had never been. "Morning, Josie," he said gently, voice warm where moments ago it had been cutting.

Lucy stared, words jammed in her throat. The sweater mocked her; a flag of ownership raised on enemy ground.

Josephine tilted her head, her smile delicate, knowing. "Am I interrupting something?"

The question was silk, not curiosity but theatre. She knew exactly what she was doing.

Edward moved instinctively toward her, hand brushing her shoulder, voice tender. "No. Nothing important."

Nothing important. Lucy could have screamed. Their marriage, their trust, her demand for honesty all reduced to nothing because Josephine had walked into the room.

Josephine's smile deepened, a faint curve that spoke of victory. Her gaze skimmed across Lucy as if she were an afterthought, a minor character on the stage Josephine now commanded. She tugged the sweater tighter around her shoulders, the gesture intimate, possessive.

Lucy's grip tightened on the counter until her knuckles blanched. She wanted to shout, to drag the truth out into the light, to tear the smugness from Josephine's face. But her throat locked.

And in that silence, Josephine thrived.

Lucy stood frozen at the counter, fingers aching from how tightly she'd gripped it. The kitchen had shrunk around her, the rain hammering the windows like applause for Josephine's performance.

She tried to find her voice, but Ed had already shifted toward his sister, his body turned away from Lucy as though the argument they had been having only moments earlier had evaporated into mist.

Josephine's eyes sparkled with amusement, and Lucy could see the deliberate provocation in the tilt of her chin, the measured innocence in her smile. She was daring Lucy to speak, to make herself look shrill, unbalanced, paranoid.

And Ed, her husband, was ready to believe it. Worse than that, he knew it was false, knew who his sister was, but was willing to live in a false reality. A lie. And force her to live the lie too.

"Coffee?" Josephine asked lightly, already moving toward the pot. The sweater slipped off her shoulder, exposing pale skin, the collarbone sharp. It was a gesture so careless it had to be intentional. "Or is that mug for show?"

Ed chuckled softly, the sound foreign after the jagged edge of their earlier exchange. "Go on, Luce, let her make it. She enjoys it."

Lucy spun on him, her voice finally unblocked. "Are you serious? After everything? After hiding her past, after lying to me, you want me to sit here and let her playhouse in my kitchen?"

Ed's smile faltered, but not for Josephine, for Lucy. "It's not a lie. It was just... too much, too soon. I was protecting you."

"Protecting me?" She laughed, the sound sharp, hollow. "No. You were protecting her. You always protect her."

Josephine set two mugs on the table, one in front of Ed, the other at Lucy's usual place. She didn't bother with her own. Then she sat slowly in Lucy's chair, draping Ed's sweater tighter around her, her gaze fixed on Lucy like a cat watching a bird exhaust itself against a window.

"Stop," Lucy whispered, more to herself than to them. She felt the heat rise behind her eyes, her chest tightening. "Just stop."

Ed glanced between them, caught, but his hand drifted, almost unconsciously, to cover Josephine's on the table. A small, almost brotherly gesture, but devastating in its weight.

Lucy saw it, and with it came the truth she had been trying to resist. She was no longer the centre of her husband's universe, if she had ever been. Josephine was.

Her voice shook, but she forced the words out anyway. "If you keep choosing her over me, Ed, there won't be a marriage left to defend."

The silence that followed was worse than shouting. Ed's face closed, that lawyer's mask of neutrality slamming into place, and Josephine's lips curved into the suggestion of private, delicious victory.

Lucy backed away from the counter. Her heart thudded in her ears, and the kitchen seemed suddenly airless, claustrophobic. She wanted to scream, to hurl the mugs across the room, to drag Ed's sweater off Josephine's shoulders with her bare hands. But she didn't.

Instead, she turned and walked out, the sound of Josephine's soft laugh chasing her down the hall.

And in that moment, Lucy knew: Ed had become Josephine's greatest weapon.

12

November 14th

The day clung to Lucy. Normally on the journey home – in her old life – she would've looked forward to leaving her work behind her. Playground drizzle, a child's cough that wouldn't quit, glue that refused to stick and glitter that stuck to everything. Now, she longed for it.

By the time she reached the house, the streetlights had come on, and the sky had the sickly yellow of a city persuading itself to give up the day. She let herself in and breathed the ordinary smell of home, laundry powder and something faintly floral, but beneath it, sharp and unmistakable, a note of her perfume. Too much of it. A ghost pressed into the air. The perfume was not, and would never be again, Lucy's.

"Hello?" she called, forcing lightness she didn't feel.

Silence. Then a soft thud overhead, closet doors speaking in their old tongue.

She climbed the stairs, bag strap digging into her shoulder, and stepped onto the landing just as her bedroom door swung wider of its own accord. Josephine stood in front of the mirror, head tilted, Lucy's scarf looped – no, knotted, as if she thought Lucy might try and wrestle it away – around her throat precisely the way Lucy wore it when she wanted a splash of colour in a dreary winter outfit. The bottle of perfume sat open on the dressing table, a damp ring blooming on the wood where no ring should be. On the bed lay a neat fan of Lucy's blouses as if a helpful shopgirl had been here.

Josephine glanced at Lucy's reflection, then at Lucy herself, as if deciding which version to address. "There you are," she said, calm as rain. "I can't keep denying it, my sweet, generous sister-in-law. I want to see what it feels like to be you; it's the only thing I've ever wanted, I think." She spoke in a dreamy, psychopathic tone.

The words landed like a hand pressed against Lucy's mouth. For a beat she could only hear her own pulse. "Take it off," she said eventually. The scarf, the tone, the trespass. "All of it. Now."

Josephine's smirk was a small, private thing. "Don't be cross. You looked so pretty in this last week." She lifted the green blouse with the soft waist and held it against herself. "See? It suits me."

Lucy crossed the room, the floorboards complaining under her feet, and grabbed a handful of blouse. Josephine didn't even flinch. Her voice came out rough. "Get out of my room."

Josephine lowered her lashes as if Lucy had turned a light too bright. "Your room?" she echoed, as though tasting the phrase. "There is no 'your' anything."

"You live here," Lucy said, "because my husband is...." Weak. Pathetic. Hateful. "Naïve, but this isn't *your* house." The edge in her own voice scared her. She put the blouse on the bed, the bottle cap back onto glass, every small reversal a way to keep herself from shaking.

Josephine watched with mild curiosity, then shrugged the scarf free with a flourish, as if granting a child her toy. She laid it on the bedspread carefully, immaculate hands smoothing a wrinkle that hadn't existed. "I'll let you change," she said, the courtesy a mockery, and brushed past Lucy, her shoulder catching Lucy's sleeve with an unmistakable firmness. The smell of Lucy's perfume followed her into the hall, too sweet, too loud.

When she was gone, Lucy closed the door and leaned her forehead against the wood. She counted to ten. It didn't help. The room glared back at her, her life displayed, appraised, handled. She gathered the blouses one by one, folding them with a neatness that belonged to someone calmer, then scooped up the scarf and went to the chest of drawers, yanking the top one open hard enough to make it complain.

She shoved the scarf into the corner, as if hiding it might turn the clock back, and her fingers struck paper. Not soft cotton, not the slide of winter tights. She stilled, then moved the top layer of shirts. There, tucked along the side of the drawer as if a careful hand had slid them in: pages. Torn neatly along the spine, edges too perfect to be accident. She took them out.

Her handwriting on the first, her words staring back at her: *She wore my dress. I felt silly and furious. Edward laughed at the wrong thing.* Another page: *He said accidents happen. He means I am dramatic.* Another: *It isn't that she wants my things. It's that she wants me, no, to be me, no, to replace me.*

Her scalp prickled. She sifted through the pages one by one, a detective handling something illicit. No blood. No threat scrawled across the lines. Worse: evidence that refused to explain itself. Someone had chosen this drawer, this very awkward, intimate place where underwear curled like secrets.

Her stomach turned. She pictured Josephine, careful fingers pressing paper flat, shutting the drawer with polite softness, pausing by the mirror to spray another mist of perfume for Lucy to find.

See me. Find me. Doubt yourself.

Lucy slid the pages back and closed the drawer quietly, as if noise might tip the house into a new disaster. In the mirror she looked too pale, the corners of her mouth pulled down when she wasn't managing them. She put her scarf on, fixed it in the mirror and saw in the gesture Josephine's earlier echo. She ripped it off again and pressed both hands to her bare throat until the thud of her pulse steadied.

Downstairs the front door opened and closed. "Luce?" Ed called, as if it was a normal day, a normal life. "I picked up wine."

13

November 19th

Monday arrived with low light and a sky the colour of wet slate. She came home after twilight and found the hall lamp already on a small, stagey glow, as if someone had been practising the moment she would cross from pavement to carpet.

Ed's study door was half open. He called it a home office but it was more like a room design to advertise his impressiveness: neat shelves of casebooks, the good printer, a desk he polished when he was anxious. Lucy stepped in to drop the electricity bill on his desk. She was constantly grateful for his desire to handle the bills.

The computer screen was awake. That shouldn't have meant anything. Screens wake. But the second she saw the page she knew something was wrong. Her inbox. Not his. Her name top right. Messages arrayed like organs on a tray. Subject lines that were hers alone: **Re: Charlotte, Homework resources, Mum's GP appointment, Mechanic invoice**. The last one opened and sitting there like a middle finger: *Brake fluid flush & refill. Cap re-seated.* Beneath, the little thread icon showing the message she had sent the garage, thanking them, asking how often a flush would be needed.

Her stomach dropped. She hadn't logged in here. She had changed the password last week to something complicated, hadn't she? She was almost sure. She'd changed it often ever since a hack a few years ago. It wasn't that she had hidden her password from Ed, but she doubted he would've known it. She moved the mouse and another tab flashed forward: the archive folder she'd made for the unknown number, the screenshot of the text glowing faintly in the thumbnail.

Accidents happen. Take care.

Her skin prickled with heat. She took a step back from the desk and then forward again because she was sick of running and pretending and, most of bloody all, ignoring. She looked at the cursor blinking inside her own sent box. Someone had scrolled. Someone had read. Someone was still here.

"You need to be more careful," Josephine said from the doorway, voice smooth. "Guessing your password was so, absurdly easy. Honestly."

The light from the landing found her cheekbone and turned it into sculpture. She leaned against the frame with casual elegance, one hand lifting to trail along surface as if testing it for dust. Her hair was loose; she wore a cream blouse that made her look impossibly innocent.

"Get out," Lucy said. Her voice was low, not the shout the moment deserved. Low sounded more like control.

Josephine's gaze slid from the screen to Lucy's face and back again. "Email is practically a diary," she said, with a knowing smirk. "You should assume everyone can read it. The world leaks, Lucy. Secrets never stay buried. A cliché, I know, but it happens to be true."

"You're impressive, and you don't scare me." Lucy stepped

between her and the desk, ignoring the shiver in her voice. "Move."

Unmoving, Josephine watched Lucy with an interest so mild it was disrespectful. "I was curious if it's only me you're so rude with," she said, eyes bright with a sick mixture of mischief and malice. "You're far more gracious with other people. It's as though I'm some monster in your eyes, Luce. Your own sister-in-law."

Lucy's hands were shaking. She tried to still them by clenching her fists, but that only resulted in trembling fists. "Out," she repeated. "Out of this room. Out of my diary. Out of my bloody email. And out of my life!"

Josephine's smile tilted, patient as a nurse, and clearly, she thought Lucy was sick. "Oh, sweet," she said, not unkindly. "You still think you stamp your feet and get your way." She took one step closer and lowered her voice to the hush of bedtime. "Eddy will always choose me over you. I'm going nowhere."

The sentence landed with the cold of a blade. Lucy felt a dark feeling settle over her shoulders. She turned and reached to the keyboard, half expecting a knife in the back, logged out in quick, staccato clicks.

Josephine's mouth pinched, barely. She lifted her hands in mock surrender. "There you go," she said, airy. "You've taught me boundaries. I am now fixed... since you seem to think I'm the broken one, not you."

"Go," Lucy hissed.

Josephine went with a loud tut, as if Lucy was the one in the wrong. Lucy stood very still in the study and made herself breathe properly. In. Out. In again. She shut the door, locking herself in, locking *Josie* out. She wished doors worked like rivers: open, and everything runs out; close, and nothing gets in.

She took a minute or two to calm herself down, to push away the vivid and tempting images of Josephine lying on her back, face broken, or crying as Ed waved his hand in her face and roared at her to treat his wife with some respect. It seemed impossible. It seemed like heaven.

Then she went to find her husband.

He was in the sitting room, sat on the sofa with a document open on his laptop and a crease at his brow that meant he was "reading" in the way that meant he mainly wanted to avoid conversation. A presenter on TV muttered quietly about sports.

"Ed." Her voice shook and she didn't hide it. "She logged into my email."

He looked up as if forced to. "Who?"

Who? Lucy wanted to scream. *What do you mean, who? What could you possibly mean by that?*

"Josephine." She spoke the name very slowly, careful not to let her anger erupt. "On your computer for some messed-up reason. My inbox was open. She was reading everything. She'd logged into the archive for the text—"

"What text?" He closed the laptop.

She held his eyes. "*Accidents happen. Take care.* From an unknown number. The morning my brakes failed." She hadn't told him before; she'd been saving the proof as a private anchor. But privacy in this house was painful. It felt more like loneliness.

His face shifted from concern to calculation. She believed for a beautiful moment her husband would finally take her side. Then the old, practised neutrality slid into place like a fist reapplying a bruise. "Luce," he said gently, coaxing, "you're winding yourself up. She wouldn't do that."

"She just did," Lucy said. "She told me my password was easy. God knows how she guessed it. You know how much I change it after that hacking crap."

Ed's mouth twitched. Amusement? Sympathy? "You do reuse, sometimes. Was it my name followed by our anniversary this time? Or your mum's birthday?"

Lucy gritted her teeth. *Oh, well done you, great guess*, she thought sarcastically.

"She said *Eddy* would always choose her," Lucy went on, driving the stake in before she lost the nerve. "Said it like a prayer. Like a threat. Like a promise."

He ran a hand across his jaw as if he could tidy thought with touch. "She's... dramatic. And you're... you know you can be,"

"Paranoid?" Lucy offered. She had never hated a word more while also wanting to cradle it, because this would all be easier if it was paranoia. It was better than the alternative, the ugly unavoidable truth that her husband was gaslighting her to her face and didn't even seem ashamed.

He frowned and Lucy was sure she almost saw a flicker of guilt. "She's a good person, Luce. If you'd just give her a chance."

"I gave her my house," Lucy said. "I gave her my place, my family, my patience, my spot on the goddamn sofa. And now my privacy. What else does a chance need? Aer you even hearing me? *She logged into my email.*"

Ed glanced at the ceiling at the sound of footsteps, Josephine moving around, a constant presence they couldn't deny.

"I want her to leave," Lucy said firmly. "Tonight. Tomorrow at the latest."

Ed's expression stiffened. For the first time, Lucy hated her husband, and hated her sister-in-law even more for making her feel this. "That's not fair."

"Fair?" Lucy almost laughed. "Fair is telling me who's moving in before she arrives. Fair is not hacking my life because you're bored. Fair is choosing your wife when your sister tries to sabotage your marriage."

He stood, too quickly, red flush creeping up his neck. "Stop. Don't talk about her like that."

"She is reading my email. I don't know how many ways I can say it."

"No, she isn't." He shook his head. "You left it open by mistake, or—"

"Ed." She kept her voice level and dropped it an octave until he had to listen. "It was in *your* study. She went into your study and hacked into my email for a sick thrill. You need to ask her to leave."

He blew out a breath and glanced at the ceiling again – at his sister really – looking like a man asking a god to change the terms of a contract he'd signed drunk. "We can't," he said finally, and we was the worst choice of word. It made her an accomplice.

"Why?" Lucy asked. "Give me one reason I won't resent for the rest of my life."

Footsteps on the stairs. Soft, deliberate. Then the doorway filled with that showbiz face, that Broadway hair, every inch of her a performance. Josephine held a mug of tea; Lucy wasn't even surprised to see *World's Best Husband* scrawled across the mug.

"I can't possibly leave before Christmas," she said, as if gently correcting a child's wild suggestion. "Eddy and I have been making plans." She looked lovingly at him. "Like we used to do, when we were young. So many wild, wonderful plans. It will be perfect."

Ed's mouth softened. His eyes glazed as his mind went elsewhere, to places Lucy clearly couldn't take it.

Lucy's blood ran cold. Christmas was over a month away. The word stretched ahead like a snowfield covering a corpse-laden battlefield, blank and suffocating. She tried to calculate the days and found she couldn't do sums with the urge to scream making her throat tight and clouding her thoughts.

"We've been planning Christmas," Ed said, with the gall to sound at least a little guilty. "Mum and Dad are off on their cruise. We thought, well, why not?"

We. She felt it land, and in that feeling something in her fully woke up. "You planned Christmas without me."

"You've been... distant," Josephine said sympathetically, as if this were a concern she'd meant to raise at a more appropriate time. "And it seemed kind to take something off your plate."

"My plate," Lucy echoed, thinking of the plates upon which Josephine had served Ed's favourite meal, thinking of the plates in the restaurant around which Josephine had humiliated her.

She looked at Ed, really looked, stripping his body down to boy, brother, man, and found each part holding a string that led to Josephine's hands. "Ask her to go."

He didn't. He sat, which was worse. His shoulders rounded, and a grim determination touched him. "After Christmas. We'll make a plan."

Josephine sipped her tea, then set it delicately on a coaster as if demonstrating how to be civilised. "We'll make it nice," she said. "Trees, lights, the whole house shining. You'll love it, Lucy. Truly."

Lucy imagined a tree in the bay window, imagined Josephine arranging the ornaments, imagined Ed laughing, imagined herself slipping in and out of the film like a continuity error. Something in her flinched from the picture like a hand from a flame.

"No," she said. "Not here. Not like this. This isn't what we were supposed to be, Ed. Not... this."

"Don't make this hard," Ed said, tired now, which made him sound reasonable, which made Lucy feel unreasonable. "Please."

Lucy thought of the dress and the perfume and the car crash which could've gone far, far worse. She thought of her diary disappearing and reappearing and the email and all of it, the big mass of Josephine, and the painful fact she was losing herself.

"I won't live like this," she said. "If she stays, I go."

Ed flinched. “That would be dramatic, Luce. Come on.”

Josephine smiled almost sadly. “Nobody is going anywhere. We’re going to have a wonderful autumn and an even better Christmas together.”

Lucy glared at them, the brother and the sister, the old team, and felt the room recede an inch, then another. She put her hand on the back of the armchair because she needed to feel something that was not moving.

In the distance a siren she couldn’t see threaded through the November cold and unravelled. She imagined for a moment opening the front door and stepping out into that weather without a coat and walking until the house could no longer find her. Instead, she set her jaw, walked to the study, and shut the door. She turned the key, the little brass one that had always seemed performative and now felt like a tool. She sat at the desk and opened the laptop to a blank document. She didn’t need the new notebook for this. She began to type: **Boundaries breached: email hacked. Threat implied. Husband indifferent. Christmas as weapon.**

Through the wall she could hear Josephine laugh softly and Ed answer with the tone he used only with her, his baby sister who could do no wrong.

14

November 26th

The afternoon folded itself into that thin winter light that makes everything look gentler than it is. Parents clustered at the railings, children ambling toward them, small hands in larger ones, the familiar jigsaw of scooters, buggies, and the excited energy of home-time freedom. Lucy stood on the top step, calling goodbyes, returning waves, performing the steady smile that says: *yes, your child is safe, yes, we'll do it all again tomorrow.*

A few minutes later, she was halfway through a conversation with a dad about a missing reading book. Then the atmosphere suddenly changed, the way rooms do when a certain person enters them. She looked up.

Josephine stood on the pavement just beyond the gate, as if she'd been placed there by a set designer who understood how to make maximum impact. Long camel coat, scarf that wasn't Lucy's but was similar, *no way that's a mistake*, lipstick toned down to a sympathetic berry. She raised a hand in a small, demure wave.

Lucy felt the recoil in her body, the flinch she'd trained

herself to hide. She finished reassuring the dad, sent him away with the promise of a fresh copy, and told herself to breathe. Maybe Josephine would stay at the edges, would, just once, not intrude. Not try to make this place, like everywhere and everybody else, hers.

Ms. Patterson appeared at Lucy's shoulder with the unerring radar of gossip. Ms. Patterson was the kind of colleague you wanted – sensible shoes, reliable humour, a middle distance calibrated for listening. "Do you know her? Is she a parent?"

Lucy licked her lips. "Josephine. She's my sister-in-law."

"Your sister-in-law? She's stunning."

"She's... visiting," Lucy said, and heard how reluctant it sounded.

Josephine had already slid through a gap in the parents and begun her model-like walk toward them. She didn't hurry; she arrived as though it was her right. "Lucy," she said warmly, pitching her voice to be heard by Ms. Patterson. "I was nearby. Thought I'd surprise you."

Ms. Patterson offered her hand, clearly charmed. "You must be Josephine. We've heard... well, we haven't heard anything, actually. Lucy keeps her home life private." She offered the devilish wink of a gossip collector. "Which is rare here."

Josephine laughed softly. "That sounds like our Lucy Luce. We're so proud of her. She works so hard, doesn't she? Dear Lucy. I don't know how she does it."

Lucy could feel the words collecting in the air around them like a swarm of bees getting ready to sting. "Thank you," she managed. She had no idea how to convincingly act grateful to the woman tearing her life to pieces.

A mother with a child in a dinosaur hat interrupted to ask where lost property was kept; Ms. Patterson pointed and threw in a cheery joke about gloves running away in pairs. Josephine used the gap to turn to Lucy fully, lowering her voice just enough. "You look tired," she said. "Are you eating enough?"

"I'm fine," Lucy said, just as a boy ran past, tripped over his own enthusiasm, and went down. She kneeled automatically, checked he was okay, sent him on with a warning to be more careful. *Bad advice. He might end up like me. Too careful.*

When she stood again, Josephine had drifted toward Ms. Patterson, who was buttoning a child's coat.

"And she never complains," Josephine was saying, eyes bright with admiration. "Even when she's under incredible strain. The job, the house, everything. I try to help. I'd do anything for her."

Ms. Patterson nodded, impressed. "She's a marvel."

"She is." Josephine touched Lucy's elbow in a way that might have read as sisterly from ten paces. "I'm lucky to have her."

Is that true, or does she just want to make her dramatic exit?

Lucky. Lucy felt the wrongness rise like vomit.

Josephine reached into her pocket and took out her phone. "Excuse me, I have a call to make." She wandered off.

Ms. Patterson pulled her cardigan closer and looked at Lucy with genuine warmth. "She seems lovely. You're lucky."

Lucy forced a smile that made her cheeks ache. "So lucky," she said, hoping Ms. Patterson didn't hear the sarcasm.

They walked to the staffroom together so Lucy could fetch the stack of marking she'd promised herself she wouldn't take home. Josephine abrupted ended her call, if it had even been real, and hurried after them. She moved through the corridors like someone who belonged there.

She's going to take this from me too, Lucy thought, terrified.

"So many little chairs," Josephine said, peering into one of the rooms. "I feel like a giant."

"Most people do," Lucy said, trying to keep her voice neutral.

In the staffroom Josephine admired a child's painting of a lopsided snowman and said, "You must love it here."

"I do," Lucy said. It was her safe space. It was her refuge. She felt ill at the sight of Josephine invading it. "Yes."

When they stepped back out into the cold, Ms. Patterson was shrugging into her coat. She caught Lucy's sleeve quickly, lowered her voice. "Invite her to the fair," she whispered. "We need glamor. She's clearly got that in spades. If she a model?"

Lucy had never wondered what it would be like to scream in kind Ms. Patterson's face before. Now, she imagined grabbing her face with both hands and roaring like a goddamn lioness.

Josephine threaded her arm through Lucy's as if they were best pals. "Shall we go home?"

Lucy slid her arm free. "I have marking," she said, holding up the stack. "I'll be along."

Josephine's smile flickered, a candle threatened but not out. "I thought you were going to take that home?"

Lucy said nothing. Just stared. *I don't want to go anywhere with you.*

"Well, don't be long." Josephine huffed. "Eddy hates eating late."

"He can eat," Lucy said tightly, "without me."

The look that passed over Josephine's face was small and triumphant. A point scored for a game Lucy hadn't agreed to play. She watched Josephine walk away, head high, and felt the ground tilt. There was only so much one woman could take.

Ms. Patterson sidled up next to her and threw an arm over her shoulder. "Cheer up, the fair is almost organised."

"I'm okay," she muttered, because that is what you say even when your life is being rearranged around and everything's turning to crap.

A while later, Lucy hung her coat on the peg, put her bag down in the hall, and stood a moment listening for what tonight would bring.

The living room door was ajar. Ed's voice came first, low, familiar. Josephine's soon followed, pitched to sincerity, soothing. *It's the way you speak to a lover.*

Lucy didn't step in. She stood in the shadow outside the door, heart thudding, and let the words come.

"I'm trying," Josephine was saying, not pleading, simply stating a truth for the record. "I make her coffee, I fold the laundry, I stay out of the way when she looks like she wants to bite my head off. But no matter how hard I try to be her friend, she won't let me in."

Ed sighed. Heavy, theatrical. "She's under stress, that's all."

He should be yelling at her. He should be reminding her of all the horrible things she's done.

"I know," Josephine said oh-so reasonably. "But it's been weeks. I worry for you. Both of you. For your marriage."

"You don't need to," he said softly. "It's just... delicate. If we can get to Christmas."

Josephine let out a small laughing exhale. "*If* we can get to Christmas? Darling, of course we can. We always get through things together. Especially Christmases, no matter what. Remember when the power went out and we ate mince pies under a blanket by the fire? We were happy with so little."

Ed chuckled, the boy version of him obediently rising up. "We were."

Lucy closed her eyes. She saw a different Christmas, just her and Ed, steam curling in the air from their mugs of hot chocolate. Maybe Lucy would even give him a pregnancy test as a present. Maybe this could've been the proper beginning of their lives together.

Josephine's voice grew softer. "You deserve someone who makes you happy."

Go to hell, Lucy thought. *Oh, go straight there, and don't pass go.*

There was the slightest pause before Ed answered. "She does," he said, but then he sighed. "She did." His voice broke. "She will." Tears pricked Lucy's eyes. She wiped them angrily away.

"Does, did, will," Josephine murmured. "But right now?" Another careful pause. "She's not herself. Paranoid. Suspicious. It's hard to live with. You shouldn't have to."

Lucy's stomach dipped, a lift falling a floor too far. The word paranoid had grown layers in this house: accusation, diagnosis, cudgel. There it was now, slipped into her husband's ear like poison disguised as medicine.

Ed's voice found its responsible timbre. "It's my marriage," he said. "I'll handle it."

Confront her. Do something. I am not mad.

"I know," Josephine said, sweet and understanding as per. "And I'll help. If you let me." She waited just long enough. "If *she* lets me."

Lucy could step in now and make a scene, insist on her own narrative – AKA, the bloody truth – shout about the email, the text, the brakes, her diary. She could force Edward to triangulate with her while the room was still warm.

Instead, she stayed where she was, feeling paralysed and so blindsided, she could hardly think. That was her main weakness, Josephine's main advantage. Lucy had never expected any of this. She wasn't ready for it. But her sister-in-law was.

It was not cowardice, she told herself, praying it wasn't a lie. It was reconnaissance.

Inside, Edward exhaled again. "Thanks for trying, Josie," he said.

"You don't need to thank me," Josephine said, too gentle.

"For what? For loving you? For loving her because you love her?" A beat. "For letting me take care of both of you?"

The audacity of it lit Lucy's rage like a match. She felt sick enough to sit on the stairs and put her head between her knees. She didn't. She stepped back from the door as if it might bite and walked, soft as she could, down the hall to the kitchen.

She turned the tap on low to cover the sound of her breathing and watched water twist down the plughole, felt her patience and her sanity going with it. She imagined every word Josephine had fed Ed settling in him. He didn't care about the truth. Only *Josie's* truth.

Lucy opened the back door and let in the cold. Air bit the skin on her forearms. Somewhere on the next street a dog barked as if announcing itself.

You deserve someone who makes you happy.

She stood in the doorway and heard it again, in Josephine's voice and then, cruelly, in her own, because precious months ago she had looked at Ed's sleeping face and thought, *I will. I'll make him the happiest man alive.* She thought it still. Maybe that was why she was holding on so desperately.

Lucy hid when she heard them emerging from the living room. Moving on instinct, she slipped into the dark of the pantry before they saw her, then peeked her head around the doorframe. Josephine emerged first, smoothing the sleeve of her cardigan, mouth arranged into thoughtful concern.

Ed followed, slow. He paused at the bottom of the stairs and rubbed his forehead. Did he look concerned? Regretful? Did he care?

Lucy could have stepped out then and said: *I heard you, both of you; stop turning me into somebody I'm not.* She stayed in the shadow and let him go past, his hand gliding along the banister, far too at ease considering what he was complicit in.

In the small study that had become a refuge by default, Lucy sat with the notebook open on the desk and a pen ready. Date. Time. Location. She wrote: *At the door. "Paranoid." "You deserve someone who makes you happy."* She underlined the last sentence once, then twice, until the ink blotted. Then she closed the book and sat very still.

Let them talk, she thought. *Let them build their case.* She would build hers. And when the verdict finally came, she would be ready.

15

November 29th

The next morning, Lucy woke early and went downstairs, feeling like a stranger in her own home. The longer this went on, the stronger the feeling became.

In the kitchen Lucy stopped. Something was wrong. She didn't move. She looked down at the broken wine glass on the floor; the red wine dried into the tiles like old blood. The shards were too even somehow, the puddle too artful. It seemed staged.

"Careful." Josephine's voice floated from the hallway. She appeared with a dish towel over one shoulder. "You wouldn't want to cut yourself. That would be a tragedy."

Lucy's breath became thin. "What happened here?"

Josephine tilted her head in theatrical thought. "An accident." Then, after a beat too small to be innocent: "Yours."

"I didn't do this."

"Didn't you?" Josephine's tone was almost sympathetic. "It was late. You were in one of your moods. You slammed the cupboard, the glass fell, you said you'd 'sort it tomorrow.'" She lifted her hands in a small, helpless gesture. “I suppose it is tomorrow.”

Lucy looked up slowly. “I didn’t do this. Not last night, not ever.”

This is their final play. Make me believe I’m insane. Lucy’s heart had begun to hammer in her chest.

She hadn’t done this, had she?

Josephine’s mouth arranged itself into profound, *believable* concern. “Memory is tricky.” She nodded toward the bin. “You also threw something away that wasn’t yours.”

A cold thread ran through Lucy’s spine. She crossed the room, nudging a safe path through the glass with the side of her shoe, and lifted the lid. On top of the rubbish, artfully arranged, a pair of silver cufflinks, Ed’s favourites, the ones his father had given him the day he qualified, a tiny E engraved in each one.

She reached in with two fingers and lifted them free. Sticky, cold.

“What is wrong with you?” she whispered, though she wasn’t sure who she meant.

Behind her, footsteps. Ed, hair damp, tie unknotted, paused in the doorway and took the scene in. “What happened?”

“She smashed a glass,” Josephine said gently. “It was an accident.”

“Stop,” Lucy said. “No.”

“And then she threw your cufflinks away,” Josephine added, soft with regret, as if only telling on her beloved sister-in-law reluctantly. “I found them just now.”

Ed looked from the shards to the cufflinks to Lucy. Doubt grew in his eyes like frost. “Luce?

You can’t be serious, she screamed in her head. *How can you even look at me like there’s a chance it was me, and not her? How, Ed?*

“No,” Lucy said again. She held the cufflinks out to him as if they could absolve her hands by leaving them. "I didn't do this. I went to bed early." She swallowed.

"That doesn't..." Ed started, then stopped. He took the cufflinks and closed his fist around them, and she watched his knuckles go bloodless. "You might have—"

"She was upset," Josephine said, stepping in with perfect timing. "Yesterday. After school. It happens."

Lucy heard the old word moving toward her – paranoid – a brand that would deform how Ed saw her. "I didn't throw them away," she said, careful, low, as if reason could be coaxed back into the room, into the house. As if there was a chance she could stop this madness. "Why would I throw away something so special to you? Something your father gave you?"

Edward flinched almost imperceptibly at *father*. The room tightened around the word. He knelt and began to gather glass into the towel, the pieces chiming against one another obediently. Josephine crouched beside him. They made a good team. Lucy watched them clean a scene she had not made.

When the last shard lay on the towel's, Josephine tied the corners and held the bundle up with a small flourish. "Sorted." She smiled at Ed, then turned the smile half a degree and it landed on Lucy like pity. "You should eat," she said. "Low blood sugar never helps."

"I'm not—" Lucy began, then gave up on the argument before it gave them more ammunition. "I really think, Josephine, Ed, please listen, I think you need to leave. Find somewhere else. Please." She hated her begging tone, but how many times could she ask for the same thing?

Josephine's eyes lit excitedly like she's got the response she wanted. "Not until after Christmas," she said brightly. "Ed and I have made plans, remember? You can be ever so forgetful, Luce."

Lucy bit into her palms with her fingernails. "It's November."

"All the more time to plan," Josephine said.

Ed stood, cufflinks now in his pocket. "Let's not do this again. It's too early."

She looked at him, really looked, hoping to find her ally, though she saw a manipulator, an abuser. Unless he truly believed Josephine's outlandish lies? Unless he thought *Lucy* was lying? "I didn't do this, Ed. I didn't do any of it. You're either blind... or you're on her bloody team."

Ed's gaze slid away. "Please," he said. "Just... just stop making me choose."

Josephine slipped past Lucy to the bin, dropped the towel in, and closed the lid with a gentle finality. "Shall I make toast?" she asked no one in particular, then answered herself. "I shall."

Lucy stared at the clean tiles where the mess had been and saw the residue anyway, the faint red stain you can't scrub out, the blood that would always be there. Even when she was gone. She felt the panic rising with no room to grow and stepped back from the counter. "I'm going to school."

Ed looked up as if she'd said she was moving out. "I'll ring you at lunch."

"Don't."

She turned before she could say anything else, grabbed her bag, and left that house full of liars and strangers.

~

She didn't drive far. She pulled into the carpark of a supermarket, wanting to be surrounded by people, by normalcy.

Her hands shook on the steering wheel; she told them to stop and they wouldn't. For a moment she did nothing but breathe, one measured inhale, two sharp exhales, trying to reset something that had been dragged off its track.

Then she called Charlotte.

By the second ring, Charlotte answered, voice automatic and bright as she said hello.

"Charlotte," Lucy whispered.

"Oh, hell," Charlotte said. "This doesn't sound good. Tell me you're parked."

"I am." Lucy pressed the phone to her cheek. "She smashed a glass and put his cufflinks in the bin. Said I smashed the glass. Said I binned the cufflinks. He didn't even argue. He doesn't want me to make him choose, apparently."

"Oh, Luce."

"She told him she saw me do it." Lucy laughed in disbelief, a sob threatening. "He looked at me like he was trying to remember the last time I told the truth."

"You didn't," Charlotte said, steady. "We are starting from there. You didn't."

"I know I didn't," Lucy said. "But my husband didn't believe me. Or didn't care. I don't know which is worse. She's staging scenes. A little wannabe Tarantino. I'm the idiot who walks in after the curtain's gone up, and everyone claps. Except I didn't even agree to be part of the show."

Charlotte let the silence hold, then spoke softly. "Do you feel safe?"

Lucy thought of the text, the brake fluid, the never-ending gaslighting. "No." The word surprised her with how easily it came. "I'm scared of what she might do next. To my things. To my life. To me."

The car's interior fogged a little; Lucy wiped the windscreen with the side of her hand, smearing it worse, then gave up. Outside, a dog trotted past in a tiny raincoat that would have made her smile a week ago.

"You can come here," Charlotte said. "Right now. We'll put the kettle on. We'll call a solicitor. We'll call the police if we must. You don't have to win a war in a house where the rules change every hour."

"I don't want to leave," Lucy said, and heard the small, furious child in it. "It's my home. If I leave, she'll say I couldn't cope. She'll turn Ed even more against me. She's already winning."

"Leaving isn't losing," Charlotte said. "It's regrouping. It's choosing to live another day with your mental health not completely in the gutter. Right now, she wants you thin and brittle and breaking. Don't help her."

Lucy gripped the steering wheel until her knuckles turned white. "If I go, doesn't she win?"

"If you stay and shatter," Charlotte countered, "she wins anyway."

"He looks at me like I'm a problem to manage," she said quietly. "If she appears like some vengeful bloody angel, he forgets any conversation we were having. I might as well be invisible."

"She's using their shared history against you. You shouldn't have to be caught in the middle, hon."

"I want to make him choose," Lucy said, grinding her teeth, a flood of adrenaline pumping into her just at the thought. "I want to say, 'me or her' and not be afraid of the answer."

"Then choose yourself first." Charlotte drew breath. "Pack a bag. The essentials. Anything you'd cry over if it vanished." *Anything Josephine will find and steal or break, you mean.* "You can stay with me."

Lucy thought of the first time she and Ed had viewed that house, fast lovers, the swirling maelstrom of infatuation and obsession not yet releasing them. They were still drugged on each other, ready for the next step, ready for the world. She saw Ed smiling down at her with the whole future gleaming in his eyes.

"I can't give her my house." Resolved thundered into her. "I can't teach her that all she has to do to win is wait until I'm tired."

"Then don't," Charlotte said. "But draw a line she can't cross. Set rules that have teeth. Locks. Cameras if you must. Witnesses. Speak to a solicitor about your rights. Tell Ed in writing what you will and won't tolerate. Write it like a teacher. Clear targets. Consequences."

A miserable laugh. "Success criteria: 'no more psychological warfare in the kitchen.'"

"If you don't say it, no one will." Charlotte paused. "And while you're saying it, while you're staying, give yourself a break. Be kind to yourself. If you need to sleep at mine to sleep, do that. You can fight for your house without living in the blast zone every night."

Lucy breathed. In. Out. She looked at her hands on the wheel, the chewed skin at the base of her thumb, the small ink mark from a leaky whiteboard pen that had refused to wash off. She imagined driving home and walking into the kitchen and finding another bizarre scene, another casual insult, more tears stinging her eyes when her husband yet again proved himself to be a stranger.

She wanted to fight, but maybe Charlotte had a point. Maybe they would break her before she got the chance.

"I'll come after school," she said finally. "One bag. But I'm not running. I'm not hiding. Just sleeping."

"Good. I'll be here. I'll be waiting. We'll make a plan that doesn't depend on..."

"On my husband picking my side. It's okay. You can say it."

"I'm so sorry, hon."

Lucy whispered, "No."

"Pardon?" Charlotte said.

Then, louder, *"No."*

"No?"

"I'm sorry, Char. I can't do it. I can't run to yours. I can't hide away. Even if it would be for the best. I just... I just can't. They won't win. They won't break me."

She hung up and rested her forehead on the wheel. A leaf slid down the windscreen, leaving a dark green signature.

At the junction, she checked the brakes out of a habit that would never leave her now. The pedal yielded, then held. She turned toward school and a day that still had demands of her children with their small catastrophes, and felt the crackling edge inside her refuse to fold.

She was teetering. That much was true. But she was not in freefall. Not yet.

16

December 7th

When Lucy got home, the house was quiet. She took some time to herself in the bedroom, reading a novel, sinking into the mattress and the quiet and pretending everything was normal. But when she heard Ed come home, she didn't wait.

She hurried down the stairs and spoke before he could set his briefcase down – before she could lose her nerve. "Put her in her place." Her voice was low, unadorned. "Tonight. Now. Or ask her to leave."

Ed paled. "Luce—"

"She's humiliated countless bloody times," Lucy went on. "Do I need to go down the list? The brakes. The email..."

"We don't know any of that was her," he said, weary. "It's a—she's—"

"She's an *ex-convict.* She's a danger! To my job, my marriage, my name."

He flinched, and there it was, the brotherly protective instinct. He shut down. The old lawyer's face. The gate dropped. "Don't," he said. "Not that."

"Then what?" She spread her hands, encompassing him, her, them, the house, his betrayal. "What can I say that you'll hear? She threw away your cufflinks and said it was me. Your wife, Ed. She lied about your wife. Doesn't that mean anything?"

She tried to kill me and mocked me in a text.

He shook his head, slow, betrayed. "I can't do this if you're going to keep,"

"Seeing what's in front of me?" She laughed; it sounded like glass preparing to break. "Neither can I."

The door opened. The third actor had arrived on their depressing stage.

Josephine folded her arms in the doorway, lipstick flawless, red hair flawless, psychopathy... flawless. She took in the tableau with practised affection. "Oh, darlings," she said, "are we have a little hallway heart-to-heart?"

"That's none of your business," Lucy said.

Josephine's mouth curled. Not a smile; something private. "That's really rather childish, Lucy."

"Enough," Lucy said sharply. "All of this is enough. You don't get to waltz in here and change everything. This is my house."

Josephine regarded her like an interesting plant she hadn't expected to grow thorns. "Your house," she said softly, as if tasting it. "You keep saying that."

Ed moved to stand between them. "Josie," he said, warning. "Please."

Finally, there was something, a scrap of support. Lucy was ashamed by how eagerly she clawed onto it.

"Please," Josephine echoed mockingly. "What? Be kind? I am kind. I've given up so much to be here. My independence. My personal freedom. To help you, Eddy, and your new wife."

Lucy's laugh was a snarling, animal noise. "You're pulling us apart and you know it."

"Or perhaps," Josephine said, tilting her head, "I'm showing you where the cracks already were."

Ed shut his eyes as if the light was causing him pain. Lucy had never seen Ed as a pathetic, weak man before. Had never dared to consider it. But now...

"Stop," he said, his new catchphrase.

Lucy felt something inside her, something flammable that had been clinging onto dear life, catch and burn. She stepped closer to Josephine so they were eye to eye. In the glass of the print hanging opposite, she saw the two of them together: her paler, gaunter; Josephine glowing like the subject in a film frame.

"You are not funny," Lucy said. "You are not charming. You are not owed this place. I don't care how tragic your little story is. You've stepped over the line again and again."

"Now wait a sec—"

"You've made my husband complicit in gaslighting me. You've bullied me. You've shamed me. You've made me a prisoner in my home."

"I don't think,"

Lucy sliced her hand through the air, stilling Josephine's words. "Here is your warning: do not do it again."

Josephine's eyes widened, delighted, as if Lucy had finally given her what she wanted. "See?" she said to Ed. "She can't help herself."

Lucy turned away because if she kept looking at Josephine's smirk she would force it off her face. She turned to Edward. "Choose. Now. If you can't, if you won't, then say that, and I'll make the only choice left to me."

He stared at the floor. A long pause. Maybe he might do the right thing. "You can't ask me to do that," he muttered, weak, defeated. "We're a... complicated family."

Josephine beamed. A human firework. "He doesn't like

ultimatums," she said, as if coaching Lucy before an interview. "You should know that by now."

"You've pushed me far enough," Lucy said, hating the shiver in her voice, the tears constantly threatening.

"Eddy, I know what you hate even more than ultimatums…" Josephine gave Lucy a wicked look, as if her true self was emerging, her real self pressing through the mask. "Ultimatums people make knowing they can't keep them."

Lucy turned swiftly, ignoring Josephine's little laugh, ignoring Ed's half-hearted plea for her to wait.

If he really wanted me to wait, if he really cared, he'd kick her out the door. He'd hold me like he did on our wedding night. He'd make me believe nobody will ever hurt me.

But Ed wouldn't ever be able to do that again, because Ed was the one hurting her. He could call it family loyalty or whatever else he wanted, but the truth was, he was turning her world to pure hell. And Lucy was complicit; that was perhaps the worst part.

Josephine was right. Lucy had made her ultimatum, but she wasn't sure she could follow through.

She still thought this marriage had a chance.

More fool her.

17

December 7th

Morning. A bad night's sleep. Lucy had the bed to herself all night. God knows where Ed had slept. *Probably with his sister,* Lucy thought. Bitterly. Disgustingly. But she thought it all the same.

The house had that aftermath hush, like a battlefield waiting for more gunfire. Lucy came down the stairs counting the beats between her heel and the next step, a private metronome to stop her thinking about the standoff, the ultimatum, the fact that Josephine had been right; Lucy was still here.

On the kitchen table sat a cardboard box the colour of old toast, its lid already folded back. Inside, tissue paper torn with reverence, a tangle of ornaments she didn't recognise: glass birds with fat, opaque bodies and clipped wire claws; wobbly stars dusted glitter; a small wooden soldier whose paint had cracked into a network of tiny maps. The box smelled faintly of loft and mothballs, the permafrost of family.

Ed stood at the counter stirring a mug with concentration as if he didn't want to look elsewhere. At her. His wife.

Finally he looked up, attempted an expression that was supposed to smooth over everything. Pretend the cracks didn't exist.

"Mum's," he said. "She found them in the attic. Apparently, she used to hang them when we were little and Josie insisted, we do it exactly the same way this year. 'The old-fashioned way.'" He pitched his voice into their mother's, fond, bossy, old money with a chip in it. "Can't say no to that."

Lucy stared at her husband in abject disbelief. So this was it, then. This was how far he was willing to go. He would gaslight her over and over until she either crumbled or ran. She wondered if this was always how it had worked in his family, two realities coexisting, no thought of what the actual truth was.

"Cup of tea?" he said, when she gave no reaction."

"Sure," she muttered, tone dead, heart dying, thoughts crumbling to ash. Dramatic? Maybe. But it was the truth.

"Herbal?"

"Why not." Her voice was dull.

She sat at the table as he made the tea. He handed her the mug nervously, eyebrow raised, seeking a reconciliation. The fact he thought they could have one without a discussion, without him making a decision, was insane.

The tea tasted off. Not the tannic bite she loved. Metallic, yes, but with a bitterness that climbed the back of her mouth and unfurled there. Chemical and chalky. Wrong. She rushed to the sink and spat it out, then turned on the tap hard, rinsing her mouth until the water ran sweet again and her gums ached.

Ed rushed over. "What?"

"What did you put in it?" Her voice came out thinner than she meant, the edges frayed by the taste. "It's... God, what did you do?"

"Nothing." He stepped back, palms up, as if he thought she was going to search him. "I made like I always do, Lu,"

"It's not the same." She turned and raised the mug to her nose, sniffed like an animal. The scent was ordinary, which was worse. She set it down carefully to stop her hand shaking. "It tastes... off."

I am not mad. You will not make me believe I am mad.

"Could be the teabags?" He picked up the container. "It's in date. Smells fine. Looks fine." He shook his head, either feigning confusion or genuinely confused. She didn't know anymore. "Maybe the stress is making it taste funny."

She just stared at him.

He frowned. "I'm trying to help, Luce."

Are you, though? Are you really?

Lucy sat at the table and put her head in her hands. She was trembling slightly. Ed sat, but not to comfort her. He looked past her to the box. "Mum says the glass birds were always Josie's favourite."

Lucy bit her lip, told herself to be strong, wondered how she had married this man, wondered if they had a chance. This couldn't be ignorance, surely. It had to be cruelty.

"Aren't they brilliant?" Edward went on. "We'll do mulled wine tonight and decorate, the whole thing. Josie's already got a system in her head."

"Of course she has," Lucy said harshly. "Of course. She. Bloody. *Has*. Why wouldn't she?"

He didn't rise to her rage. Or sink to it. "It'll be nice," he said. "We could use nice."

Lucy almost mentioned that it was too early to decorate, but what queen Josie wanted, queen Josie got.

Her stomach rolled. The box on the table leered like yet another intruder. She stood abruptly and picked it up.

"Lucy?" Ed moved instinctively to keep, like a man reaching to catch a falling glass.

"Recycling," she snapped. "We'll make our own memories.

We don't need these." She lifted the box against her hip and shouldered the back door with so much force it opened violently and slammed against the wall.

Cold hit her face, bracing. She crossed the patio in four angry steps and flipped the lid of the recycling bin. Cardboard and wine bottles peered up as though curious, maybe wondering if this crazy-looking lady had lost her mind. Maybe she had. But they'd pushed her to this.

She started to tip the box.

"Luce," Ed muttered, standing off to the side, weak and unassuming. Not the man she married. Not the life she chose.

A flash of silver at the top of the bin clicked her anger into focus. Not foil from chocolate or the neck of a bottle. A flat, blistered sleeve: the kind that holds tablets by little domes of plastic you press a thumb through. Empty. Ten tidy ovals where pills had once been, pressed out clean. The cardboard backing was stamped with a name she didn't recognise.

Lucy set the ornament box on the ground, forgotten, and plucked the sleeve free with two fingers as if it might burn. She turned it over. The back gave her more data: dosage, take one at night, avoid alcohol, may cause drowsiness.

Her mouth remembered the taste of her tea again, that bitter iron with a chalk behind it. Her stomach lifted. She searched through her mind and wondered if she'd tasted that before. Buried in meals without realising it.

"Luce, what is it?"

She looked up at the kitchen window and saw her own face reflected, pale, hair wrong, a woman who wasn't the main character in a story about her life. She discreetly replaced the packet and stood, shaking her head. "It's nothing," she said, laughing humourlessly. "Whatever I say, Ed, it'll be nothing to you."

Lucy stormed into the kitchen, knowing Charlotte was right,

knowing she had to leave. A sick thought struck her. What if it wasn't Ed who had drugged her, but Josephine?

"I'm glad you changed your mind," Ed said, returning with the box of ornaments in his arms, cradling them carefully like a baby. "Josie will be thrilled. We can all decorate together. Like a family."

Lucy massaged the bridge of her eyebrows. "Where is she?"

"Upstairs. Shower." He checked his watch and, by reflex, the hall as if his sister might make one of her typically dramatic appearances. "I've got to go in for a bit, but I'll be back by four. We'll do the tree at five. Okay?"

"It's too early for decorations," she said.

"We disagree, Luce. Living with family is about compromise."

"I might as well not even speak. It makes no difference anyway."

Ed had the nerve to slam the front door when he left. Lucy hated the way she flinched, the reverberation moving through the house, through her too-tight chest.

Lucy stood and went outside, taking the pack of medication from the recycling bin. Inside, she read it again. *Do not operate machinery.* She snorted softly at warning and thought of a moving car, a red light, a brake that had hesitated. Then she thought of the taste in her mouth and felt nausea flare, hot and disloyal.

Halfway up the stairs she felt her knees loosen. She gripped the banister and told her legs to behave. At the landing she paused. The bathroom door was open, showing the misted mirror; the hallway carried the scent of shampoo she had learned to associate with Josephine, her fiery red hair always perfect. The spare room door was ajar in the way of a stage set.

Lucy didn't knock. She walked in.

Josephine was at the dressing table, head bent, towelling her hair into that orchestrated disarray magazines call effortless. She wore a silk robe and an expression of anticipation and self-assurance. She met Lucy's eyes in the mirror before she turned.

"Morning," she said.

Lucy held up the tablet pack. "What's this doing in our recycling?"

Josephine didn't even blink. She glanced at the pack, then back to Lucy's face, her expression never shifting. "Pills in a cardboard pack," she murmured. "In a recycling box intended for cardboard. Sharp, aren't you."

"They're empty."

"That's how pills work," Josephine said, friendly. "You take them, they're gone."

Lucy stepped closer. Her own pulse sounded ridiculous in her ears. "My tea tasted wrong."

"Did it?" Josephine widened her eyes in a parody of concern. "Perhaps your milk's off. Eddy does let things linger."

"It tasted poisonous." The word landed and startled the room before it startled Lucy. "Metallic. Bitter. Like someone put something in it. I don't take milk in my herbal tea. But somebody might crush up a tablet, open the bag a tiny bit, put some in there."

"They're my pills," Josephine said, voice low and patient as if Lucy were a child who'd suggested something ridiculous. "I have trouble sleeping. You try being me in this house." She lifted one shoulder. "Stop being paranoid."

There's that word again. That bloody word. Lucy tried to calm herself down, but she was hot all over.

Lucy took the last step between them until they were close another to touch. "Did you put anything in my tea?"

"No," Josephine said. "If I wanted you gone, Lucy, you wouldn't be here to argue with me."

Everything inside Lucy went very cold. The sentence sat

between them as a declaration of absolute fact. She couldn't feel her knees for a second.

"There it is," she said. Her own voice sounded foreign, thin and measured and belonging to someone who had woken from a long, deep sleep. "There you are."

Josephine's smile deepened, almost affectionate. "We're done with theatre, then? Good. It takes so much energy to pretend."

"Leave," Lucy said. Screw a broken record. She didn't care if she was repeating herself. She needed this devil out of her home. "Today. Pack your things. You don't live here. Not anymore. Never again."

Josephine tilted her head. "Eddy wants me here."

"He wants peace. That's why he puts up with your crap. That's why he... goes along with it."

But that seemed far too tame. He wasn't just going along. He was actively participating. He was fuelling it.

"He wants me," Josephine said simply. "If you can't see that by now, I don't know how to help you." She stood without haste, the silk robe skimming into place as if it had been trained. "If you make him choose, you will lose."

Lucy's wanted to melt against her sister-in-law's poise, her confidence, her fire. Instead, she stood up straighter. "I am not afraid of losing something I don't have."

"Oh, darling," Josephine said softly. "You still have yourself to think of."

"Pack a bag," she said, each syllable a nail she was perfectly willing to hammer into Josephine's coffin. *Metaphorical or not.* "By tonight."

Josephine moved past her toward the landing, close enough that Lucy could smell her skin beneath the perfume. She filled the doorway, turned.

"You're very brave when there's an escape route," she murmured. "Less so now."

Lucy showed her teeth. Not a smile. An animal flexing. "Try me."

Josephine laughed, sounding genuinely delighted. *It's all a game to her.*

"I just might," Josephine said, then walked down the hall humming a tune.

Lucy stood in the spare room breathing air that felt like poison. She set the tablet pack on the dressing table and pressed her finger hard on the name until the ink didn't smear. A fake name? She should've asked Josephine, but the answer was clear and her sister-in-law would've just lied, anyway.

She left the room and walked past the bathroom, the door now closed. Josephine sang loudly from inside.

In the kitchen, the box of ornaments waited, patient and sure of its future. She put both hands on the lid and slid it across the table to the far end, purposefully not looking at it.

Lucy put the tablet pack into a zip pocket of her bag, behind her passport, beside her notebook. Before closing it, she added entries to her notebook. The tea. The taste. The decorations. She zipped it shut.

She tried to close her mind too, just for a few moments, to get some small relief from the nightmare that was her life. But she couldn't. She was in it.

She put the kettle on, deciding she wouldn't make tea. In fact, she threw out her herbal tea. Was it possible that she'd just had an off teabag by mistake? Or was her theory plausible: that Josephine had crushed a pill and put it in?

Was her sister-in-law really that far gone? Was Lucy an idiot for even asking that question after everything?

18

December 8th

Lucy came upstairs with a basket of clean towels hugged against her ribs and stopped at the landing because the air pressed colder there, a temperature drop like a warning. The spare-room door stood ajar. Not *the* spare room. Not Josephine's room. This was the other one. The door they kept closed.

She could not remember the last time that door had opened. She and Ed had filled it in a week's flurry of hope and love. They had planned and held each other tightly as their future glowed inside them. Lucy set the towels on the landing table quietly, as if sound might attract attention,and reached for the door with a hand that didn't look like hers. Everything was distant, alien.

The smell found her first: lavender, clean cotton. A sweetness with an oldness to it. She pushed the door, and it moved as though reluctant.

The nursery no longer had a thin layer of dust. It looked too clean. And yet the cot looked like it had once belonged to a baby... not that they were waiting for one, planning. A mobile spun slowly, moon and stars chasing each other. Pale light glowed through the thin curtains.

A soft toy sat propped in the corner: a rabbit with drooped ears and a face stitched into the kind of mildness people think babies like. Another rabbit on the dresser, bowed toward its twin as if conferring. And a picture of a rabbit on the wall. On the chair, a neat pyramid of folded baby clothes, sleep suits with stubby feet, a knitted cardigan, a hat with ears. The labels were still on some of them.

Lucy took three slow steps. The room shifted around her, expanding and contracting like breath. Its potential made her ache.

The bundle was a doll. Lifelike. Not the cheap, screaming plastic kind that looks like a novelty; something heavier, a vinyl mimicking of flesh. Fingernails, lashes too dark, a mouth pursed into silence. It had weight. It had life. Whoever had wrapped it had tucked the corners the way nurses do, a perfect demonstration of care.

Lucy's breath snagged. She did not touch it. She would not touch it.

A part of her, the teacher part, the woman who reassured frightened children by showing them how things worked, wanted to poke the doll, to prove that it wasn't real. It wouldn't suddenly leap up and grab her.

Relax, Luce. Jesus.

She saw her life taunted here: the doll asleep without sleeping; the bed smoothed into a caricature of what she wanted so badly. What she might never have now. Someone, and Lucy was certain she knew who, had done this to mock her. To hurt her.

Josephine. Of course. No one else would have this sadistic insanity in their messed-up souls. Unless it was Ed. Unless her husband was even more of a stranger than she realized.

Lucy's mind turned uselessly, a kaleidoscope refusing to give a picture. Why? What did it mean? Josephine's fantasies had always been about replacing, about stepping into costumes that belonged to Lucy. This was new. Or was it? Perhaps this was the final middle finger. Josephine had event taken her fantasy of having a baby, of being a mother.

On the dresser, someone had placed a silver frame. It held an ultrasound image, a print-out, glossy, a blur of white on black with the neat legend of measurements and dates. Lucy bent closer. It wasn't a real scan; it was a sample image – the kind of stock picture clinics pin to a board, the baby-in-the-abstract. Anyone could have bought it. Anyone could pretend.

Lucy told herself to breathe. She told herself to turn around and walk out and close the door and find Ed and put this in his hands and say, *see*. But when she turned, she found the doorway already occupied.

That was how she would remember this woman, Lucy realised, if she was ever rid of her. Hovering in doorways. Never all the way in, never fully out.

Josephine took the scene in with a quick glance, then her eyes were on Lucy, bright and patient, and finally she let them travel, lazily, to the bed.

"Oh," she said softly, the vowel a caress. "You found us."

Us. The word slammed painfully into Lucy. Josephine stepped inside without asking and crossed to the cot. She reached down with a trembling hand and stroked the doll's head with two fingers, a gesture so eerie and strange, Lucy was certain this sicko had done it before.

"I always wanted a baby," she whispered, not to Lucy, a revelation under her breath. "What's the harm in that?" She lifted her eyes, met Lucy's stare, and let the smile eddy to the corners of her mouth. "Just because *you* don't have a maternal bone in your body..."

The sentence almost choked Lucy.

Lucy's field of vision went narrow, then too wide, then settled on Josephine's hand as it moved rhythmically over the doll. She stroked it as though it truly needed comfort and she was the only one who could give it, the perfect mama bear.

"I don't understand," Lucy said. "What is this? Why are you doing this? Why, Josie?"

It was the first time she could remember calling her *Josie*, as if this preview into her full madness had made them more intimate.

"A nursery." Josephine smiled as if she were explaining an obvious joke to a child. "Every child deserves one. It's how you manifest a future."

"This is not your house," Lucy said. "This is not your future."

Josephine's smile softened into pity so convincing it could have been love. "Eddy and I used to play mummy and daddy when we were small. We stacked books and pretended they were houses. Used pillows for our children." She bent her head and kissed the doll's forehead like a benediction. "We were so happy in the world of make-believe... because we believed, Lucy, we believed and we – we... we loved." She croaked out the last word.

Lucy stepped back because, frankly, she was terrified. Bone-deep fear ran through her. She hit the chest of drawers with her hip and the sharp jolt was far too painful. "Stop," she said, and speak any louder.

"Stop what?" Josephine asked academically, as if she wanted to write it down. "Wanting? Imagining? Practising?" She straightened then, smoothly, weight shifting. And for a moment the room belonged to the two of them equally. "Eddy wants children," she added meaningfully, staring with wide-eyed intent at Lucy. "It's one of the few things he has never changed his mind about. He wants children, Lucy, pretty little babies with pretty little heads with pretty little bobs of red hair."

It took Lucy a second to find air. "You and your *brother*," she said, and the word made the room's temperature drop another degree. "Talk about... having babies? That's my future, Josephine, not yours."

Ed doesn't talk about having babies with his sister, Lucy thought, praying it was true, no longer sure. *I can't let her make me believe that.*

Josephine folded her hands, looking like a HR agent come to deliver bad news. "I talk about *the* future," she corrected gently. "You shouldn't try to steal it. That's not very nice. What would you say to one of your little rugrats if they tried to take something that didn't belong to them?"

Lucy's legs decided to move before her mind made the decision. She made it to the landing table before she had to stop. Beneath her hands the wood felt too smooth, treacherous, the grain hiding what it knew. Every part of this house has watched Josephine. The very structure had betrayed her.

It's thoughts like these that will make people you're nuts, Lucy cautioned herself. *Calm. Down.*

She kept going. Down the stairs, counting each step, breath still coming hard. In the hall she grabbed her phone from the bowl and went to the front room where the signal was the strongest. Her thumb found the contact.

He answered on the third ring in a short, clipped tone. "Hey."

"You need to come home," she said. No preface. The words shook and she let them. "Now. You need to see something."

"I'm working," he said dismissively. "What is it?"

"She's in the nursery," Lucy said. "*Our* nursery. We don't go in there, Ed. It's for the future. Clothes. Toys. A doll. A *doll*, and she's treating it like a baby." She heard her words and knew they sounded outlandish. But this whole bloody ordeal had been bizarre from start to finish. If it ever *would* finish. "Ed, it's wrong."

On the line, silence. He sighed after a long pause. "Luce."

"No," she hissed, fist clenched around the phone. "Not this time. You come home and you look. You don't tell me I'm tired. You don't tell me it's a joke. You *look*."

Another breath. He lowered his voice, and she imagined him checking the office, checking nobody could overhear his conversation with his apparently insane wife. "I can't leave now. Work is a mess. I'll be back by seven. I'll look then. We'll..." Another world-weary sigh. "We'll talk then."

She shut her eyes. "I don't feel safe with her," she admitted. "I'm going to Charlotte's. I'll come back when you're home."

"Luce," he said again, softer, and on another night, in another reality she might have felt the tenderness in it. "Please don't make this—"

"Difficult?" she snapped. "It's not me, Ed. It's *her*."

And it's you, she thought, but kept that to herself. Just in case they could salvage this marriage.

She ended the call before he could form a rebuttal, could drift into gaslighting and lawyer speak. She stood for a moment with the phone warm in her hand and felt nothing under her feet and then too much. Upstairs, a floorboard answered a floorboard as if in code. One she would never know.

She grabbed her bag. Coat. Keys. She moved toward the hall like a woman fleeing a fire, checking as she went that she was not leaving pieces of herself behind. At the foot of the stairs, she glanced up. She thought of the doll tucked up in the cot and felt perversely jealous. It was safer than Lucy.

She opened the front door, and the winter air rushed her. She stepped out and pulled the door behind her until the lock bit. On the step she stood for one breath, then another. The street was ordinary with bins tucked back into their places, a child's plastic scooter collapsed under a hedge, a neighbour scraping frost off a windscreen with a loyalty card, but the ordinary had acquired edges.

She walked fast. At the corner she turned and didn't look back because if she did she might see the upstairs window curtain shift, might see Josephine's pale watching face. She fled the house, but it was with her. It was inside her; she carried it. The doll with its unforgiving face. Josephine's hand smoothing the hard skull. *Us*, she had said. *You found us.*

At the end of the road, Lucy stopped and put her hand flat against the dashboard to steady herself. Her phone vibrated with a message from Charlotte: *Yes. Come. Tea on. Door open.* Lucy looked back down the street and thought, *I am not running from my home.*

This was a chance to reset. To vent. It wasn't a retreat.

Above her, a crow landed on the lamppost and gave a single caw, a sound that always made children in the playground laugh. Lucy didn't laugh. She left the car, squared her shoulders, and walked into the cold.

19

December 10th

Dusk had the colour of old bruises when Ed's car turned into the street. Lucy was waiting on the pavement, coat unbuttoned, breath clouding in pale bursts. She had walked the block three times and then stopped herself at their gate so she wouldn't look like a person in the grips of a panicked mania. When he cut the engine, the sudden quiet made the whole road seem smaller somehow.

He got out with his work face still half on, hi jaw set and tie loosened. "Luce," he said, wary. "You could have waited inside."

"I didn't want to." Her mouth was dry. "Come on."

She had spent the afternoon at Charlotte's and then come home without going inside. She had been afraid to enter her own home. The truth of that stung her.

He followed her up the path, keys jingling in his hand. She moved through the hall and they went upstairs. The landing light flicked on with a click that sounded louder than it was. It was like she was waiting for an explosion.

The nursery door stood exactly as it had that afternoon:

almost closed, almost open, neat as a line in an exercise book. Lucy pushed it.

A room. Just a room. The curtains fully open. The doll was gone. Tucked up and taunting her. *Did you seriously expect her not to move it?*

Lucy stood in the doorway, stomach dropping like a lift with a cut cable.

Ed looked past her shoulder, then stepped in, frowning at the mobile, the moon and stars moving slightly. "What am I looking at? It's our nursery, Luce. Our beautiful nursery."

"Nuh-no," she said. "She had a doll in here, Ed. She was treating it like a baby. She told me..." Lucy stumbled, gripped the wall, and Ed rushed to her and offered his arm. She clawed far too desperately, hungry for warmth, for human comfort, for *him*. "She said you and her talked about having babies."

Ed took a step back and put his hands in his pockets. He shook his head slowly. "This obsession with Josie has got to stop. She talked about having babies... with me? Her brother? Luce."

She waved her hands, heat rising. "She did," she said, her tone as fiery as oh-so sweet Josie's red hair. "A doll. Acting like it was real. Or some weird religious thing of worship. She..." Lucy could hear how frantic she sounded, how unhinged. She raised her voice. "She kissed its head!"

He looked at her as if she might need help. "Oh, Luce."

"She did it," she repeated. "I went to Charlotte's. She had time. Obviously, she wasn't going to bloody keep it here. I should've thought. I should've taken a photo!" She swallowed, felt the cold panic run its hand down her spine. "She covered her tracks. She knew you'd take her side."

He rubbed his eyes, thumb and forefinger at the bridge of his nose, an old habit that used to make her want to kiss him and now made her want to shake him by the shoulders until his bones shattered. "I don't see a doll," he said. "I see our nursery. I see hope. I see our life. That's all."

"Because she moved it."

"I've got no way to prove or disprove that, Luce."

"I'm telling you she moved it," Lucy screamed, the veins in her neck bulging.

She fled the room into the hall and began tearing through the house as if the doll was a living thing and was actively hiding from her.

She ran around, loudly, stupidly, doors banging open, the house creaking and groaning in protest. Kitchen cupboards, the utility closet, the understairs, the pantry. She found nothing but the lived-in debris of the same life Josephine had been stealing from her. No doll. She couldn't search Josephine's room – *my spare room* – because she had locked it.

Ed waited in the landing, apparently feeling she had to get this out of her system. When she finally collapsed against the wall and slid down it, sitting like a little kid with her legs stretched in front of her, breath coming too fast, he finally knelt, put his hand on her shoulder.

"Lucy," he said gently, "you're scaring me."

"I'm scaring *myself*," she said. Her voice was too high. She made it lower. "Ed, listen to me. She's gaslighting me in real time. She..." She couldn't go on, because what if he was in on it too? How could he *not* know what was going on?

He put a hand on her upper arm. His palm was too warm. "You need to stop. You need to breathe. You need to, God, Lucy, calm down."

The phrase was a match on petrol. "Don't," she said. "Don't ever tell me to calm down."

I'm the only one who gets to tell me to calm down.

He released her. His own calm hardened into something mean. "You sound, I'm sorry... you sound like a lunatic."

The word split something. She felt the tear happen, clean and quick, the way fabric goes when it's been holding on for too long. She stared at him long enough to memorise the exact shape his mouth made around *lunatic* so she could hate it properly for a long time.

"Right," she said, standing and walking toward the stairs. "I need time to think."

"Where are you going?" He sounded ever so slightly protective, then annoyed at his own instinct to be. "It's dark."

"It's darker here." She took the stairs slowly. No rush. No panic. No mania. She wasn't shouting. She wasn't begging. Inside, her heart was a tight vice and her emotions were a battlefield. But she wouldn't let him see. "I don't feel safe with her. I don't feel safe with you believing her. I'm going for a drive. At least nobody will try to mess with my head in my own bloody car."

"Don't be dramatic," he snapped after her.

She pulled on her trainers and opened the from door. Cold air came in like relief. He followed her onto the step. "Luce," he said, a plea and a scold. "Please. Stay. We'll talk when Jo's,"

"When Jo's what?" she snapped. "Finished tearing me apart? Taking my place?"

He didn't answer, and that was all the answer she needed. She walked down the path and was at the car, unlocking it with a beep that sounded far too cheerful for a night like this.

"Text me," he called, ridiculous in the doorway, a man playing the husband part far too late and far too timidly.

The engine turned over. The radio woke and she killed it. She pulled away from the curb, hands at ten and two like a learner, and didn't look in the mirror until the end of the street. When she did, the house sat there, square and decent and lit, windows like calm eyes.

We could sell it. A family could live there for years without knowing what happened inside those walls.

~

The quiet in a car after you turn off the engine is never complete. Plastic ticks as it cools. Outside: wind in winter hedging, a lorry far off complaining about its life. *I know the feeling.* She put her forehead on the steering wheel and let the world be still for a few moments.

Am I losing my mind. She didn't ask the question; she didn't dare. She saw the doll again, heard her sister-in-law's sick words. She felt the clean, deliberate emptiness of the room with Ed beside her, and the word *lunatic* sprung like a mousetrap between them. She saw Josephine's face as she declared that she and Ed were going to have red-headed babies, and her world felt like it was spinning too fast.

She laughed, then the laugh turned into a sob. She bit it back and breathed in through her nose the way the counsellor had taught her after the miscarriage: count four, hold four, out six. The memory came alive for the first time in months, uninvited, a ghost with cold hands. The day in the bathroom, the absence that stole a future they hadn't told anyone about yet because they'd wanted to keep that little slice of beauty and hope to themselves for a while. They were right to be cautious, it turned out. She put her palm flat on her stomach as if it were a torch she could relight, and then lifted it, shame stinging like nettles.

Josephine would fill a role meant for her. Ed had stood there, in the nursery, knowing her pain, and had still taken his sister's side.

Her phone vibrated against her thigh. For a second she imagined Ed, contrite. The screen lit up her face; she saw herself in the black window, a woman lit from below like she was telling a campfire story. A ghost story with a bad ending, probably.

Unknown number.

She opened the text because not opening would be cowardice, and that hadn't got her anywhere so far.

Sweet dreams, love from mummy.

The words took the skin off her. Cut her soul. A photograph bloomed in her head uninvited, the doll in the cot, a cot meant for her baby, her life, her future. Lucy was supposed to be the *Mummy* in this story.

More sobs gripped her. The little animal noises that tell the body the threat is too big to swallow whole. Pain and humiliation and the specific grief of being called mad by someone she loved. The message sat on the screen like a taunt.

When the sobs ebbed, she wiped her face and waited for the shame to arrive. It didn't. She stared at the message until the words detached from meaning and then swam back.

This wasn't just about Ed. It wasn't even about the marriage, not tonight. It was about erasure. The nursery had been a rehearsal, a set, a threat. The message proved it. *Sweet dreams.* Sleep. Don't notice. Don't wake up. *Love from mummy.* Not *mum*, not *mother.* Josephine had chosen the word the way a surgeon chooses an instrument.

Lucy breathed. Count four. Hold four. Out six. The car ticked gently, loyal, the only thing that was these days. She thought of the blister pack in her bag and the doll's hard lips and the way her husband hadn't even considered taking her side.

She typed without overthinking, forcing her thumbs to be steady now: **I know it's you.** She sent it to the unknown number and watched the blue bubble land. No reply came. Of course not. Josephine had made her mark.

She put the phone face down on the passenger seat and sat in the dark long enough to feel her heartbeat step down a floor.

Then she started the engine, not because anything in her had decided to become brave, but because she had do something.

She pulled out, kept to the slow lane. At the roundabout she didn't indicate left for home. She indicated right towards Charlotte's and felt, as the indicator tick-ticked its tiny metronome, a mean, bright seam of anger held her together. Not fear. Not collapse. The narrow, necessary anger that lets you keep going when the past is tearing you apart.

Mummy, she heard in her thoughts. *Mummy, Mummy, Mummy...*

20

December 10th

Charlotte opened the door before Lucy knocked properly and pulled her in, arms tight, no questions first. The kind of kindness that reminded Lucy she was loved.

"Shoes off," Charlotte said, adorably bossy and kind. "Takeaways on the table. I ordered everything."

The living room was a warm island, lamps low, sofa inviting, a laptop open like a second hearth. Paper napkins. Chopsticks perched on cartons. The sight made Lucy's knees almost fold in relief. She stood for a second with her hands on the back of a chair before remembering how to sit.

"Tell me," Charlotte said, giving Lucy her full attention.

Lucy told her. The nursery, which was supposed to be sacred. The doll. Josephine's hand on the vinyl head and the whisper – *mummy* – that had invaded Lucy's phone. The blister pack. The tea.

"And when he came home?" Charlotte asked. She already knew what Lucy was going to say, her expression pitched into pity already.

"She moved it," Lucy said. "because of course she did. And then he looked at me like I'd dragged him to a gallery of my own bloody insanity. Her side, obviously. Always her side."

Charlotte swore under her breath. She slid the laptop closer, typed in her password with command and care, then pushed cartons toward Lucy. "Eat. I won't hear a word until there's food in your belly."

"I'm not hungry."

"You are," Charlotte said. "Chicken, Noodles, extra spring rolls because I like to watch you judge me as I wolf them down."

Lucy managed a mouthful. Her body surprised her by receiving it. Halfway through she realised she was starving and let her fork go into autopilot.

Charlotte ate too, quietly, both of them focusing on their food because it was easier than everything else. When Lucy finished, Charlotte sat back. "Stop trying to convince Edward," she said. "You need to make a decision."

Lucy blinked. "Maybe that's what I'm afraid of."

"You keep approaching him like a pupil with an essay you want good marks on. Giddy, hopeful he'll see sense. You need to get the grade *then* approach him with a big fat A, so you can say, look, I've done it. Here's the proof. I'm quite sane, thank you very much."

Lucy smiled tiredly. "Easier said than done. But you're right."

Charlotte tapped the laptop's trackpad and the screen woke to search results: audio recording tips, legalities, discrete apps that hid as calculators on phones, dictaphones disguised as pens. "You're in your own house. You can record conversations you're part of. In this country, that's allowed. Just don't publish. Keep it for your solicitor." She glanced up. "If it comes to that."

"It's probably past that," Lucy said. "I'll do it. I think... I've got no choice."

Charlotte reached across the table and put her hand on

Lucy's wrist. "Good. And—" She hesitated. "This is awful to say aloud, but his sister's obsession with him is... unhealthy. Unnatural." She didn't say the word they both heard anyway. It hung in the air, heavy as a curtain you can't see through.

It's plain bloody weird, Lucy thought. *It's borderline incestuous. I know, Char.*

Lucy felt nausea rise. She nodded. "I know."

Charlotte squeezed, firm. "Be careful. She has history. The other girlfriend—" She didn't finish because neither of them needed to hear it aloud. "If she did it once, she can assault someone again."

"She will," Lucy said quietly. "Or she'll try." Then, stubborn: "Unless I stop her."

Charlotte held her gaze. "Then you stop her with evidence. It's time to stop being so nice. No offence, hon, but it's time to stop being so... Luce. You sleep here tonight. Edward can wallow until morning."

Maybe he'll feel guilty, she thought stupidly, hopefully. *Maybe tomorrow, everything will be different.*

Lucy pictured the bed, warm and safe. But then she shook her head. "I have to go home. I have to end this."

"If you go, you have to take action," Charlotte said firmly. "You leave your phone on. Voice memo ready. Tape anything. Everything. If you feel yourself getting shaky, call. I will say unhelpful practical things like 'breathe' and 'leave' and you will thank me later. I'm serious, Luce. I should be screaming at you to call the police, really. I should force you to stay here."

Lucy laughed this time properly, the sound surprising both of them. "A cheeky wrestle after a takeaway, huh?"

Charlotte laughed too, but her eyes were sad.

"We were happy," Lucy murmured. "When I met him. It was like something out of a film. I felt so special, so seen, so unique.

Then Josephine waltzed in and suddenly he only had eyes for her."

"Lucy," Charlotte said, and the gentleness had teeth. "You were happy because it was the two of you. Then it wasn't. I'm not sure,"

"We can get it back," Lucy cut in, hoping it was true.

She took out her phone and found the voice memo app, then decided to download a second one instead, one that looked like a calculator and wouldn't get her caught. She tested it, recording the sound of Charlotte laughing, then the rustle of the takeaway bag, then a whispered "I can do this, Lucy, tonight," which sounded like a stranger because the woman's tone was almost brave.

Charlotte stood reluctantly. Lucy knew she wanted her to stay. Lucy had *come* here to stay, and yet each time she fled her home, it felt like a defeat. It felt like it was pulling her back.

I can do this. I'm strong enough.

At the door Charlotte hugged her again, longer. "If she corners you, don't shrink," she said into Lucy's shoulder. "Stand proud. Stand tall. It's *your* home, hon. And," She hesitated.

"And what?"

Charlotte pulled back. "He doesn't get to call you mad again. If he tries, walk out mid-sentence. It'll train him to be better."

"You think he's *trainable*?" Lucy asked.

"Like a badly behaved golden retriever," Charlotte said. "He needs commands... if he likes being bossed around by his sister, be even bossier."

Lucy rolled her eyes. "I'm not sure if that's possible."

~

The house looked composed when she returned, curtains drawn, a windowed smile of domesticity that would photograph well. Lucy stood outside a few moments and watched her own breath in the porch light, then slipped the phone out of her coat pocket, pressed the disguised record button, and slipped it into her trouser pocket. She checked once the screen blank, app hiding as a calculator, then opened the door.

In the living room, the television flickered artificial snow across handsome faces. Josephine curled on the sofa like a woman who had invented comfort, one leg tucked, blanket arranged to advertise softness. Ed's navy jumper slouched on her frame as if it had been tailored to make her look like his lover.

She looked over, smiled with absent affection that felt practised. "Back so soon?" she asked.

Lucy stepped into the room and the phone kissed her thigh through fabric with every movement. She took the armchair. She kept her voice level. "Where's Ed?"

"Asleep." Josephine popped a kernel of popcorn, chewed. "He was tired after the scene you caused. I told him I'd lock up."

Lucy let the sentence sit. The television's volume ticked downward as a couple on the screen kissed in tasteful soft focus. "I want to talk," she said.

"Oh, goody," Josephine said, not looking away. "I love a bedtime story."

"The diary," Lucy said. "The nursery. My car brakes." The last word felt like touching a socket.

Josephine considered the popcorn bowl. "You really should stop spiralling," she said. "It's bad for your skin. You looked all flushed"

"You moved my diary. Hid it. Returned it. I think you did it because you get a sick thrill out of it. Out of making me believe I moved it myself. You want to make me doubt myself."

Josephine tipped her head. "I don't need to make you do anything. You're doing a very good job alone."

"You invaded our nursery, played a sick game in there," Lucy pressed on, because the only way through was through. "You wrapped a doll and stroked its head and called yourself—" She couldn't say it. "You sent me a message. You mocked me. *Sweet dreams*, you said."

Josephine smiled the small, closed lip smile she used for people she disliked. "You really shouldn't check your phone while driving. Dangerous habit."

"Just tell the truth, Josephine," Lucy said, surprisingly calm. "If you're capable of that."

Josephine's eyebrows lifted. "*Brakes?* Do you seriously think... Darling, the drama." She licked salt from her thumb and looked once, lazily, at Lucy's trouser pocket as if she could see through fabric and apps.

Does she somehow know? Am I giving it away somehow? Lucy tried to act normal... which, in turn, made her seem more abnormal probably.

"You won't win," Josephine said easily.

"Win what?" Lucy asked, almost conversationally.

"Him," Josephine said, and this time she grinned, showing those neat teeth. The grin altered the room's temperature. "He'll never believe you. He belongs to me. Always has and he always will."

The sentence landed like a blade laid flat, cold, deliberate. Lucy forced herself not to look down at her phone. She let the quiet hold for a count of three, the way she did in class after a student gave an insightful answer.

Then she nodded once. "Thank you."

"For what?" Josephine feigned innocence expertly; the doll would have admired her.

"For telling the truth," Lucy said. "You've been building up to it for weeks."

Josephine tipped a few more kernels into her mouth. "It

didn't take weeks," she said. "It all began and ended the night I came home."

She said this with a dreamlike, eerie quality, as if she was reciting some religious incantation.

Lucy stood, her pulse fluttering like she'd just survived going undercover. "I'm going to bed," she said. "With my *husband*."

Josephine's eyes sparkled. "Good girl."

"Don't call me that," Lucy hissed, annoyed at herself for letting the crack show. But there was only so much she could take. "If you walk into our room while I'm sleeping, I will call the police."

"There she is," Josephine murmured admiringly. "Our little warrior."

"Save your pet names for your doll," Lucy snapped.

The hallway felt too long, the stairs, too loud. On the landing she paused, pulled the phone from her pocket with care, stopped the recording, and saved it. Her fingers shook. She played it quietly, phone cupped to her ear. *He belongs to me. Always has and he always will.* Josephine's voice came thin and perfectly through the speaker. Lucy's skin crawled.

She named the file – *Jo_confession_1* – and backed it up to the cloud.

In the bedroom, Ed slept on his side facing the window, covers half-kicked, the small complaint at the corner of his mouth that always made her want to hold him and never leave. In sleep, he looked the way he did when his love was uncomplicated.

Lucy stood at the foot of the bed for a long moment, deliberating. She could wake him, press the phone into his hand, play the sentence and watch disbelief and support captivate his expression. Or him melt into an apology. The truth was though, she was tired. She wanted her husband's warmth, even if it was fake.

She put the phone on the bedside table on her side, screen down. She undressed in the quiet, the small physics of zips and cotton sound enough to make her real to herself. She slid beneath the covers and let the bed take her weight. The sheet was cold where his warmth hadn't reached yet. She turned onto her side and faced his shoulder blade, that familiar piece of him that had once been a promise and could be again.

For the first time in weeks something that wasn't fear moved inside her. Not joy. Not safety. A flicker, small as a match struck in cupped hands: *evidence.* Tomorrow it could be a seed, a lever, a wedge. She could show Charlotte; she could show a solicitor; she could show Ed after coffee in daylight.

In the morning, she would begin the work. Tonight, she let the match burn a little longer in her hands and was careful not to blow it out.

21

December 11th

Lucy woke to the kind of quiet that feels deliberate. A wedge of winter light sat on the ceiling like a cold hand. Ed's side of the bed was empty and cooling; the dent in the pillow had already begun to forget his shape. No note on the bedside table. No text on her phone. Just the residual warmth in the duvet and the smell of his shower gel faint in the air.

She lay still and listened. The quiet was almost welcome. She took her time getting up, pretending it was a normal day, a normal life.

Downstairs, the house had dressed itself while she slept.

In the sitting room, the tree she had refused, because refusing felt like the only power left, stood in the window like a visitor with perfect posture, lights obediently threaded, branches occupied by lights and ornaments. Not her white and silver. Old glass birds perched by wire claws, belly-heavy and complacent; the glitter-dusted stars; a wooden soldier painted into a network of tiny maps where the paint had cracked. Tinsel looped around the lower branches. The angel on top had been repaired at least twice, glue peeking along the hem of its dress like a secret.

Underneath, a skirt of red felt lay exactly cantered. A string of paper chains that were childish and precise, draped the mantel. A bowl of clementines, a plate of ginger biscuits, a candle called Firwood. The room had become a card. The card did not require Lucy's signature.

Josephine had decorated while Lucy slept beside her husband. In Lucy's home. *How much can one bloody woman take?* Her head throbbed.

On the coffee table lay the ornament box she had meant to put in the recycling, its lid neatly folded back as if to say: *nice try*. A small, white tag tied to the tree's lowest branch made a quiet speech in a tidy hand"*The old-fashioned way.*" She didn't need the signature to know whose hands had tied it there.

Lucy picked up a glass bird and felt the cold of it press into her palm. She put it back. The old anger rose, less like fire now and more like pressure or a steady climb, and she pivoted, crossed the hall, and took the stairs fast enough that she tripped onto the landing.

Josephine's room looked exactly like a brochure for tidiness: bed smoothed, cushions placed like show items, dressing table arranged by height and shine. A glass of water sat on a coaster, not sweating. Nothing messy. The neatness itself loud.

Lucy checked the doorway. She moved, quick and efficient, searching through the room, careful not to disturb anything. She wasn't even sure what she was looking for. Her breath came quickly and panic tried to make her stop. Or go even further. Not just search, but destroy.

She crouched, palms to the floor, and felt under the bed. Boxes: shoeboxes that sang their brand names, a plastic crate with winter scarves. And, further back, a rectangle whose edges bit. Metal. Her fingertips found a handle.

She hauled it out into the light.

A locked box: office-grey, ugly, determined. The sort of thing that looks like it belongs in a boot, under a seat, at the back of a drawer nobody opens. The keyhole stared up at her like it was going to wink at her.

Keys. She scanned the room, the dressing table's little bowl, a tray by the lamp. She took three keys from the bowl and tried all of them. The third fit. It was almost too easy.

The lid resisted a moment, then gave.

Newspaper clippings first, pressed into a thick stack and held with an elastic band. The headline on top felt like being slapped again, though of course Lucy knew what kind of monster she was living with.

LOCAL WOMAN JAILED FOR VIOLENT ASSAULT. A smaller subhead: **Attempted murder charge after partner's ex-girlfriend found with life-threatening injuries.**

A photograph in the middle – the kind they always run, a school portrait stolen from a social media account, a smile offered to a better day. *Becca*. The name unclenched something and then made it worse. Lucy had heard it once, pronounced too quickly, pressed into a story about "an ex" who had "moved away," delivered like it wasn't important.

Another clipping:

SENTENCE HANDED DOWN IN CASE THAT SHOCKED COMMUNITY.

The judge's mouth mid-admonition, the same stock image of the courthouse steps. A column inch quoting a witness: *"It was an obsession. We all saw it."*

Letters, next, on prison stationery, the paper thin and insulted. Some in Josephine's unresolved hand, some addressed to her. *Dear Jo... We are praying for you... This will pass... You must do the work...* Others, official: visiting hours, appeals, the enumeration of rules about shoes and underwire. A printed email folded in thirds, Susan's voice. *We will not let this define you. Family looks after its own.* Lucy read the line twice and felt a small, cold fist form in her throat.

Did that mean Lucy wasn't part of the family?

Photographs beneath, a fat envelope spilled into the bedspread. Ed as a boy: gap-toothed, jam-smeared, performing at a sports day with a medal around his neck, one arm thrown around a red-haired girl who would later commit herself claiming Ed for herself and herself only. The two of them in a paddling pool, naked in the confident way of children, water catching sun. Halloween and Ed as a skeleton, Josephine a witch, both of them staring like conspirators.

More recent. Ed graduating, the cap making him look like the picture of success; a family Christmas with Susan holding a sherry, Henry in a tie, Josephine pressed to Ed's side, her lipstick a bright stripe in a room of beige. Photos of Lucy and Ed too on their wedding day, Ed's hand on Lucy's waist, the weight of vows still hot. Another: Lucy and Ed in the kitchen of their new home, this home, with a bottle of champagne on the counter. And then Lucy's stomach turned. There was another wedding photo again, smaller.

Her face was scratched out. Not once, not in a childish X. Scratched. A thrumming of lines until paper fluff caught under the nail of someone who had meant to erase her hard.

Lucy imagined Josephine in a rage, frothing at the mouth, ranting as she erased her sister-in-law.

The room went bright around the edges. Lucy placed the photograph gently before she tore it apart. She slid another picture free. Becca who was beautiful, with small intelligent eyes and a sarcastic smile and Ed at a barbecue. Ed laughing toward something out of frame while Becca looked at him with pure adoration. No scratches here. Not this one. That punishment had been saved for Lucy.

She reached for another clipping, then stopped. Reading them all would be like falling into a well. She restacked the papers deliberately, and looked again at the thin letters printed on thin prison stationery. *HMP St. Bride's* in block at the top of one page. *You can't imagine how loud it is at night.* Another: *Your appeal will depend on contrition.* Another, an official form half-completed – *Release Date:* blank then filled; *Probation Officer:* stamped; *Address to be Resided At:* Keaton family home, brother's residence.

That meant that Josephine had come straight from prison to here. That meant that, as far as the prison service was concerned, this was Josephine's permanent residence. Lucy closed her eyes for a moment, steadied her breathing. It was one thing after another after another after...

Calm, Luce. Think.

Lucy realised she needed to take a photo of the picture with her face scratched out. She was taking out her phone when Josephine cleared her throat form behind her.

Her cheeks were lit with cold or sick pride. She took in the scene: bed, box, Lucy's hand mid-photo; the tilt of the photograph stack. Her eyes brightened.

She stepped forward and slammed the lid shut with the flat of her hand. The sound hit the air like the report of a small gun.

"Go through my things again," she hissed, voice low and terrifying enough to belong to angry animals, "and you won't live to regret it."

Lucy's body registered the sentence before her brain. Knees loosened, stomach went thin, a bolt of ice under the ribs. Her mouth, miraculous, still worked. "You scratched my face from that photo. You... poor Becca. It's not enough that you went to prison for hurting her, but keeping her photo... Why, Josephine?"

"Ancient history," Josephine said flatly, "and nothing to do with you."

Lucy felt a surreal feeling grip her. A voice screamed loudly in her head, maybe Charlotte, maybe herself, maybe both. *What the hell are you still doing here? Why won't you quit?*

"You tried to kill her," she said, and was surprised to hear how flat it sounded, as if it was a normal part of Lucy's new existence. "You're going to do the same to me, aren't you? You're going to try."

Josephine tilted her head. "Attempted," she said at last, with the exactness of a solicitor. "Such an ugly phrase, don't you think? Attempt. As if lives were exams."

"You're playing with me," Lucy said. She could hear her heart. The sound blurred the edges of the room. "You didn't attack Becca in a fit of cold rage, did you? I bet you planned it. I bet you enjoyed it. I bet you let it build like you're letting *this* build."

A flicker in Josephine's eyes. A challenge. "Then leave, little duckie."

Lucy set both hands on the box and felt the cold of the metal leach into her palm. "Why keep this?" She nodded to the box, Lucy's scratched-out face inside. "Why carry a graveyard around with you?"

Josephine made a small noise of impatience. "Souvenirs," she said. "We all have them. Yours are your feelings."

"You threatened me," Lucy said. "Again."

Josephine leant forward until Lucy could see the pinprick reflections of herself in both of Josephine's pupils. "A warning is not a threat. It's a favour." She lowered her voice further, a whisper just bigger than a breath. "And don't pretend you don't have the answer. Would you like me to spell it out? L-E-A-V-E. Easy as teaching your little ones, right?"

Lucy's hands tightened into fists. She almost wanted this to come to blows.

But I'd lose. The thought struck her with ugly truth. *She would kill me.*

"Get out of my way," Lucy demanded, voice nowhere near as tough as she would've liked.

"This is my room," Josephine said softly. She took the box and slid it under the bed with the heel of her hand as easily as a magician returns a dove to its pocket. "And you've done enough poking around."

"How can *you* say that? After everything?"

"If by 'everything' you mean your mental decline, I'm not sure how to answer that."

The words went in, and they hurt, and Lucy let them sit like a thorn. "I'm done being polite," she said. "Leave. Today."

Josephine giggled. "Oh, silly girl. Leave, leave, leave. You're very repetitive. Has anyone ever told you that? Only of us is going to stay. If you still think it's going to be you, you're not as clever as you think."

Lucy almost fought. Almost. Almost took a swing. Her throat was tight. Josephine stared with that animal excitement like she was ready.

Lucy moved to the door. Josephine stepped aside, not much, just enough. Close enough that Lucy had to turn to avoid brushing.

"Sweet dreams," Josephine said as Lucy passed, the same words from the text, yet more proof of what this psycho had done. *Was* doing, every single day.

Lucy walked. She put one hand on the banister so she didn't lose her footing. In the hall, she pulled her phone from her pocket and called Ed. It rang longer than it needed to. He answered on the edge of irritation, probably in a meeting or doing something else that was so much more important than his wife.

"What is it, Luce? I'm in the middle of—"

"She has a box with my photo in, my face scratched out," Lucy said. No preamble. No softening. "There are photos of Becca too, Ed. The woman she assaulted. Photos so she can relive it. Souvenirs, she called them. *Souvenirs.* I found the clippings, the letters, her release papers from prison. In a locked box under her bed. The address she was released to was here." Lucy bit her lip, waited for him to speak. "She thinks she's going to stay here forever. She's going to hurt me, Ed. *Hurt* me. Do you care? When did you stop caring?"

He exhaled. Bothered. Impatient. Not the man she married. "This isn't the time."

"It's never *not* going to be the time when she's here," Lucy said.

"Lucy." He put her name in his courtroom voice, the one that thinks it can rearrange facts by rearranging tone. "All of this, Josie and her past mistakes and whatever trinkets she decides to keep for herself... it's family business."

"No," she said. "It's my business. You married me into it. You let it live in my house. It reads my diary and poisons my tea and sends me weird texts *and cuts my brakes*, Ed. Why don't you care? Did you ever love me?"

"Stop," he said, as if she had said something obscene, as if she had made a good room dirty. "We'll talk later. I have to get back to work."

"She threatened me," Lucy said. "Again. She said I wouldn't live to regret going through her things."

He made a noise, pity, annoyance; on phones they use the same muscles. "Josie doesn't do well when people don't respect her boundaries."

Lucy laughed. Lucy screamed. Lucy sobbed. It was a hybrid

noise, choked, disbelieving. "*Boundaries?* I've got a recording of her saying I'll never win. I'll never take you from her."

"Later," he said, almost gentle. "I'll be home at six. We'll sort it then." A pause, the administrative grace of bureaucracy: "Please don't make this worse."

He hung up before she could tell him there was no worse, only their new life, the one he seemed intent on living.

She lowered the phone and looked toward the sitting room. The tree blinked with automated cheer. Upstairs, a door shut softly. The house was putting its pieces back where it liked them. Soon, it would spit one of them out. Lucy should've let it be her. She should've accepted defeat.

But when she pictured Josephine's superior smirking face and heard her victorious giggle, she knew she couldn't. She had to fight.

In the pit of her stomach, something tightened. There had been moments when she'd thought this might have a happy ending. But now, living in this upside-down world where gaslighting was the norm, she knew that was wrong.

If something didn't change, and chance soon, this was going to end in blood.

22

December 11th

Lucy didn't remember the walk from the car park to Edward's office. The sky had bruised itself into a low grey, and she must have crossed streets, pressed buttons at crossings, passed other people with their bags and takeaway cups, but it all dissolved into the single, sharp conviction that she would no longer wait for him to come home, to feed her half-truths at the kitchen table.

She strode to the receptionist with the kind of determination that wouldn't accept anything else that exactly what she bloody wanted. "I need to see Edward Keaton," she said, voice tight. "Now."

Something in her face that resembled panic mixed with civilised fury, cut through protocol. The receptionist blinked. "I'm afraid I can't—"

"I'm his wife," she cut in. "It's serious."

The receptionist nervously gestured her toward the corridor.

Ed's door was half open. He sat behind his desk, tie loosened, papers in half-stacks like obedient children… children they might never have now. He looked up, startled, and began to stand.

"Lucy. What are you...?"

She pushed the door fully open and shut it behind her with a click that sounded final. "Sit," she said. Her hand already trembled as she dug her phone from her bag. She pressed play on the recording.

Josephine's voice filled the office, low and certain: *"He'll never believe you. He belongs to me. Always has and he always will."*

The sound was tinny, but unmistakable. The silence afterward swelled until Lucy thought the books on his shelves might start to lean in to listen.

Ed sat back down heavily. His face had drained, then filled with colour, then drained again. He rubbed his mouth with his hand, buying time.

"Well?" Lucy demanded.

He shook his head slowly, as if her phone had tried to trick him. "You provoked her."

Lucy's stomach dropped. "What?"

"You know what she's like when she's cornered." His voice was low, tired. "She's unstable, yes, but she's still my sister."

"She admitted it." Lucy's voice cracked. "She as much as told me she's trying to replace me. You can hear it."

Ed stood abruptly, circled his desk as if the office walls could shield him. "You don't understand," he said, and his voice cracked in the middle. "You don't know what she's been through. What it did to her."

Lucy froze. The way he said it was different. The whole room shifted, the air rearranging. She sat down in the chair opposite his desk because her legs had lost the ability to hold her. Her bag slipped to the floor with a small, lonely thud.

"Then tell me," she whispered.

He looked at her, eyes dark, jaw tight, as though he had held this secret so long he'd become part of it.

Ed leaned against the edge of his desk. His hands opened, closed. He didn't look at Lucy as he spoke; he was staring into the past.

"We were teenagers," he began. "Fifteen. Sixteen maybe. Jo," He stopped, swallowed. "She was raped."

The word hit the Lucy like a fist. Her breath caught. "Ed..."

"She told me weeks later," he continued. "By then the boy was bragging about it. Everyone thought he was untouchable. He was older, bigger. His father a drunk, his mother gone. Teachers ignored him. Police didn't care. But Jo," He dragged a hand over his face. "She couldn't sleep. Couldn't eat. She just kept saying I had to make it stop."

"Oh, Ed," Lucy whispered, and despite everything, she thought of little Josie, red hair in disarray, tears streaming down her cheeks.

"One day after school, I waited for him by the river. I told Jo to stay back. She hid in the trees. I just wanted to scare him. I swear it. I said I'd teach him a lesson."

Lucy could picture it, the skeletal trees, the flat grey water, Ed a boy with fists he didn't yet know the weight of.

"I hit him once," Ed whispered. "One punch. He went down. His head hit a rock on the bank. The sound," He flinched. "It wasn't supposed to happen. He just...stopped moving."

The room was suddenly too small. Lucy's pulse hammered in her throat.

"Jo came out from the trees," Ed went on. His voice thinned, as if the words had been corroding inside him. "She took my hand. She looked at him, then at me. And she said, 'You're my hero. He deserved it. We'll put him in the water, and no one will ever know.'"

Lucy's world, which was already upside-down, tipped some

more, became something unknowable. So this was why, then. This was the rope that bound brother to sister. It was something Lucy would never be able to compete with.

"She helped me," Ed said. "We pushed him in. The river took him. We walked away." His eyes met hers at last, and they were glassy with a species of guilt that was also devotion. "She owes me. I owe her. That's why—" He gestured helplessly. "That's why everything is the way it is."

Lucy's body had gone cold. Not just guilt. Not just family loyalty. Complicity. A pact sealed in river water and silence.

She saw her own scratched-out face. She saw Josephine's hand on the doll's head. She saw Ed as a boy, and Josephine calling him her hero while they stood together over a body.

The office spun a fraction. Lucy pushed back her chair, the legs squealing across the floor.

"Lucy," Ed said. His voice was desperate now. "It was an accident. I never meant,"

She didn't wait to hear the rest. She couldn't.

The corridor outside was too bright, the carpet muffling her footsteps as she walked faster, then faster, until she was through the double doors and outside in the brittle air.

She didn't recognise the man she had married anymore. Worse, she wasn't sure she ever had.

Ed was blind, yes. But not by choice. He had chosen to stand in the dark and keep her there with him.

Lucy walked toward her car, the icy air biting her skin, and felt utterly, entirely alone.

23

December 11th

The Keaton family house glowed like a painting. Warm yellow light spilled across the gravel drive, wreaths adorned each sash window, and smoke curled from the tall brick chimney. Inside, Lucy knew, there would be pine garlands pinned to mantelpieces, bowls of clementines shining in polished brass, and logs snapping in fireplaces. A Christmas postcard, precise and smug, daring the world to believe in perfection. Weeks had passed in a blur, one gaslighting episode to the next, with the rush of school causing the days to blur into each other.

It was late November somehow; time had skipped. Late November and the days still rushing, this new abnormal normalcy taking hold.

Lucy pressed the bell. Its sound echoed faintly through the hall, followed by deliberate footsteps. Susan opened the door, wrapped in a cashmere cardigan the colour of bone. Her expression froze when she saw Lucy.

"Lucy." Not a welcome, not quite a reproach. A neutral word, spoken with edges.

"I need to talk to you. Both of you." Lucy's breath plumed in the cold. "Please."

Susan hesitated long enough to make her point, then stepped aside. "Henry's in the drawing room."

The drawing room was lit with firelight and lamplight. A Christmas tree stood tall in the bay window, dressed in red and gold, each ribbon tied with practiced hands. Henry sat in a wingback chair by the fire; newspaper folded on his knee. He looked up as Lucy entered, expression unreadable.

"Lucy," he said, voice as flat as his wife's.

She stood in the centre of the rug, heat from the fire touching her legs, and tried not to let her voice shake. "I need you to listen. Josephine, I think she's dangerous. You have to intervene before something worse happens."

Henry cleared his throat, eyes flicking briefly to Susan before returning to the fire. "Dangerous is a strong word."

"She is dangerous," Lucy pressed. "You've seen what she's capable of. You can't keep pretending she's just eccentric or fragile. She's poisoning my marriage, my life. She set up a messed-up nursery in my house. She spiked my tea. She reads my diary. She cut my brakes, for Christ's sake."

Susan perched on the arm of Henry's chair, hands folded neatly, her face controlled. "Josephine has suffered enough. She served her sentence for what she did to Edward's ex, Becca. Her time is done; now it's time for her to live"

The fire popped, making Lucy jump. Susan and Henry exchanged a glance, quick but dense with shared history.

"You knew," Lucy whispered. "What she was. What she's capable of. You knew she hadn't changed."

Susan smoothed her cardigan, eyes cool. "Of course we knew. We support her, as any family would. To you she's all these..." She waved a hand as though it wasn't important. "Things. But to us, she's just Josie."

Lucy's throat burned. "Support her? She tried to kill a woman. And you supported her? How could you possibly excuse that?"

Susan's lips pressed into a thin line. "Because we know the whole story. Something you don't."

"Then tell me!" Lucy's voice cracked. "Tell me what justifies her obsession, her cruelty, her violence!"

Susan's voice sharpened, brittle crystal. "She was a child, broken in ways you cannot imagine. That boy. What he did to her,"

Henry shifted, his gaze fixed on the fire. His fingers tightened on the armrest.

Lucy's stomach lurched. "Ed told me," She said carefully. "About the fight after school. About the river."

Silence. Susan's jaw clenched. Henry reached for his glass, took a slow sip of whisky, and still didn't look at her.

"About what he did to the boy," Lucy went on, and Susan and Henry flinched as though the memory hurt them, but there was no surprise.

"You knew," Lucy repeated, louder this time. "And you said nothing to me. Nothing, all this time, nothing. You let me marry into this. You didn't stop to think, *Will she fit? When our precious Josie is out of prison, will she* let *her fit?*"

Susan spoke at last, her tone clipped. "Edward did what any good brother would. It wasn't just that our sweet angel was raped, Lucy. She was a child... and he took her, defiled her. And the rape... God help me." She covered her mouth for a moment, choking a sob. "It resulted in a pregnancy. Thankfully, she had a miscarriage."

The words landed like a stone dropped into Lucy's chest. "Thankfully?" she choked. "That's the word you use?"

Susan lifted her chin, her eyes cold and steady. "Do you have any idea what it was like for her? For us? To hold her together while she shattered? To watch her try to put her life back piece by piece? And then you come here, after everything, demanding we turn our backs on her."

"I'm not asking you to turn your backs," Lucy said, voice trembling. "I'm asking you to see her clearly. She's not the broken child you're describing. She's a manipulative, dangerous woman who's destroying my life."

Henry shifted again, still avoiding her eyes, as if he could survive the past by refusing to acknowledge it. Lucy saw Ed in him then, the way he retreated, the habit of pretending everything was okay, stubbornly believing it as though sticking to a religious creed. She heard Ed, all the *calm downs* and the *not nows*, the never-ending avoidance.

"What about Ed?" Lucy demanded. "What about that day after school? That boy, if he did what Josie said he did—"

"Excuse me?" Susan hissed.

"If he did it," Lucy went on, thinking, *and there's a chance he didn't, let's be real. This is Josephine we're talking about.* "Didn't you stop to think about the effect that might have on him? On his future relationships? On his relationship with his sister?"

Henry's glass rattled faintly as he set it back on the table. "It was a long time ago," he muttered.

Lucy stepped closer, hands balled at her sides. "A long time ago? A boy died, Henry. He died, and Ed and Josephine hid his body. You buried that with the rest of your secrets. And now you expect me to carry it too."

"Enough," Susan snapped, her voice ringing against the polished walls. "We will not discuss this in that way. We protected our children. We kept this family together. And we will continue to."

Lucy's heart hammered. "At what cost? Ed attacking someone to protect his sister isn't normal. I know it's... it's heroic, maybe. It's the right thing. It's what people claim they'll do when somebody hurts someone they love. But it must've had an effect. It caused a a storm, Susan and Henry. A storm and I'm in the middle of it."

They exchanged a glance, seemed to hesitate a little.

"And Josephine's obsession with him is unnatural," Lucy went on pleadingly. "You know it... you must know it."

Susan's mouth pinched. She didn't deny it, but she didn't confirm it either. Henry finally looked at Lucy, his gaze tired, hollow, then away again.

"Please," Lucy begged. "You're his parents. You could stop this. You could tell Ed the truth. You must see it. She uses him. She manipulates him. She turns him against..." *Me.* "People he shouldn't be turned against. You could show him what she is."

Susan's expression softened only slightly, but her voice stayed firm. "Edward already knows what matters. He will never abandon her. Nor will we."

Tears pricked Lucy's eyes, frustration and fear clashing in her throat. "Then what about me? What about your son's wife? Don't I matter? Don't you care that she's trying to erase me from his life?"

Susan's face hardened again. "You should go."

The fire spat, sparks bursting then dying. Lucy's fists clenched tighter. The truth was out, naked and foul, and still they stood around it pretending it was family.

"You'll regret this," she whispered, though whether to them or herself, she couldn't tell.

~

The air had shifted by the time Lucy stepped out onto the gravel. The light had thickened into dusk, stars pressed like pins into the hard sky. Her car sat at the edge of the drive; its windows filmed with frost. She was outside her own home, yet she felt like she was standing outside a stranger's house.

The door clicked behind her.

Josephine stood in the porch, coat open, red hair shining in the glow from the porch light. Her face carried the smug calm of someone incapable of losing.

"They called you," Lucy said, flat.

Josephine stepped onto the gravel, slow, deliberate, her boots crunching like punctuation. She leaned close enough that Lucy could smell the faint sweetness of wine.

"You'll never win," she whispered. "How many ways do I need to explain, Luce? He'll never choose you. And neither will they."

The words cut like wire. Lucy's breath stuttered, rage trembling through her bones, but she bit down hard on it. She would not give Josephine the reaction she wanted.

Josephine's smile widened, satisfied by the silence. "Good girl."

Lucy turned and walked to her car. The keys shook in her hand as she unlocked it.

For the first time, she felt the fury crystallise into something sharper, cleaner. She was done playing defence. Done reacting, done begging for scraps of loyalty from people who had already chosen their side.

She drove to a nearby service station and sat under the bright lights, drinking black coffee, letting the caffeine buzz through her body, letting it harden her resolve.

As she drained the dregs from the mug, the liquid scorching her throat, Lucy made herself a promise.

She would go on the attack. And Josephine would never see it coming.

24

December 11th

The drive home was a blur of frost on windshields and headlights that split the dark into violent stripes. Lucy barely registered the route she knew by heart; her mind replayed Susan's cold face, Henry's evasive eyes, and Josephine's triumphant whisper on the drive. By the time she reached the house, her chest ached with the weight of betrayal.

Ed sat sprawled on the sofa, his tie gone, his shirt half-buttoned, a tumbler heavy in his hand. He looked exactly like his father. His cheeks were flushed with drink. He didn't look up when Lucy entered. Neither did Josephine.

Josephine hovered close, perched on the arm of the sofa. She had slipped Edward's cardigan over her shoulders, as though she were wearing his very skin. She leaned in too close. With every pause in the music, Lucy heard the glug of whisky pouring, Josephine's hand steady on the decanter.

"Another," Josephine murmured, topping up his glass before he could even ask. Her fingers brushed his knuckles as she passed it back.

Edward laughed, a sloppy, boyish sound that made Lucy's stomach turn. "You always know what I need, Josie."

Lucy froze, staring. She felt invisible. Dead. Horror thickened her throat. Ed leaned further into Josephine's touch, as though her presence was gravity itself.

Lucy tried to breathe, to steady herself, but the sight carved into her like glass. Her husband, her Ed, looked as though he belonged to someone else entirely.

"Ed," she said, her voice tight.

He blinked at her as if remembering she existed. His smile faltered. "Luce. You're back."

Josephine didn't move away. She swirled the whisky in her own glass, eyes locked on Lucy over the rim. Her smile was small, private, victorious.

Lucy's chest tightened until she thought she might choke. The lamplight made everything obscene: Josephine's hand on Ed's shoulder, his half-slumped body leaning into her, the Christmas tree blinking cheerfully in the corner like a witness too polite to interfere.

"Get your hands off him," Lucy snapped.

Josephine tilted her head, feigning innocence. "I'm just keeping him company. He was lonely."

Ed groaned, dragging a hand over his face. "Christ, Luce, not tonight."

"Not tonight?" Her voice cracked like a whip. "You're sitting here, letting her paw at you while you drink yourself stupid. Do you even see how wrong this is?"

Ed slammed his glass down hard enough the liquid splashed. "Don't start."

"Don't start?" Lucy took a step forward, rage shaking her bones. "She's replacing me in front of you, and you're too blind or too drunk, or too bloody screwed in the head, to care! You need to get away from her. You need to let me help you. You *both* need help."

Ed lurched to his feet, unsteady and furious. His face was blotched red, his eyes glassy. "You're insane. She is my sister. My *sister*. And you twist it into something filthy because you can't stand that she needs me."

"She doesn't need you. She *owns* you!" Lucy screamed. "She's poisoning you, Ed. She's been doing it for years. And you're letting her."

Josephine's hand rested lightly on his arm. "Don't, Eddy. Don't waste your breath. She's not herself."

The dismissal stung, though it shouldn't have. Lucy should've been long past that. Her breath came sharp, ragged. "You're both disgusting."

Ed stared at her for a long moment, swaying slightly, then shook his head with contempt. "I can't do this." He shoved past her, shoulders colliding hard enough to make her stumble. The front door slammed behind him.

The silence afterward was worse than shouting. Lucy stared at the doorway, her mouth falling open, struggling to believe what had just happened, though again, none of this should've been a surprise. He had run just like before.

At least he made some bloody noise this time, Lucy thought in disgust. *At least he pretended to be human.*

Lucy turned back slowly. Josephine remained where she was, one leg crossed over the other, glass in hand, light painting her cheekbones sharp. She looked perfectly at home, as though she had been waiting for this moment all along.

Josephine rose gracefully, setting her glass on the mantelpiece with a deliberate click. The smile she wore was no longer one meant for witnesses. It wasn't civilised. It was like an animal flashing teeth.

"You won't last here," she said softly, almost tenderly. "The last one didn't."

Lucy's throat tightened. "Becca," she whispered.

"He's mine. So why don't you do yourself a favour and leave, before I'm forced to make you. Like I did with Becca. I've given you so, so, *so* many chances. Are you stubborn, sweet sister-in-law, brave, or stupid?"

The words hung in the air, thick and toxic.

Lucy stumbled back a step, her spine brushing the Christmas tree. She could smell the whisky on Josephine's breath as she stepped closer, closing the distance between them with feline grace.

"You're sick," Lucy whispered, though her voice trembled.

Josephine's face came so close Lucy could see the tiny flecks of malice in her eyes, could smell the wine layered beneath the whisky. "Sick enough," she murmured, "to finish what I start."

Lucy's body screamed at her to move, to flee, but her legs held her in place. The tree lights blinked mockingly, red and gold shadows stuttering across Josephine's face.

Josephine reached out and touched the sleeve of Lucy's coat, her fingers light, possessive. "Think about it, Lucy. You've already lost him. The sooner you accept that, the easier it will be."

Lucy jerked her arm free, heart hammering. "You'll never win."

Josephine laughed, low and throaty. "Sweetheart, I already have." A pause, then Josephine suddenly threw her hands up. "Boo!"

Lucy threw herself back violently, letting out a panicked cry. She almost fell with the force of it. Josephine cackled, stared, unmoving, unblinking. And for the first time Lucy understood Josephine wasn't bluffing, wasn't simply cruel; she was deadly.

And she was running out of time.

I should've seen who she really was the day we met. I should never have left it get this far.

"I'm not scared of you." Lucy regretted the words the moment she spoke them.

Josephine laughed again, no words needed. She knew Lucy was scared of her. And she liked it.

25

December 12th

The house was too quiet when Lucy opened her eyes. Not the peaceful kind of quiet, but the sort that prickles across the skin, warning of something already broken. She rolled over, reaching instinctively for Ed's warmth, but the bed was cold beside her. Memories rushed back in.

Her husband, a killer. Her sister-in-law, a killer. Her new family, liars, avoiders, gas lighters. All of them. And yet she was still there.

I can save this, she thought as she sat up. *I can save us.*

The air carried a faint metallic tang that didn't belong, like copper coins warmed in a palm. Her body knew before her brain did: blood.

The floor creaked as she padded across to the landing. Somewhere below, something crunched, brittle and unnatural. Her nerves became taut. She moved slowly down the stairs, one hand on the bannister, listening.

The smell grew stronger.

At the bottom, she stopped dead.

The kitchen was a scene from a nightmare. Shards of glass were scattered across the tiles, glinting viciously in the weak morning light. Not a simple accident, the debris was spread too wide, as if someone had swept their arm across a counter, shattering deliberately.

And on the counter itself streaks of red. Not a spill, not ketchup. Blood, smeared in uneven swipes as if a hand had dragged itself along, marking territory.

Lucy's lungs caught. She stepped closer, instinctively hugging her arms around herself. Every muscle screamed that the tableau was staged, a message carefully written.

Then voices.

She froze in the doorway, peered around the edge. They were stood at the end of the hallway, half turned away from her.

"...she came at me in the night," Josephine's low voice murmured, heavy with rehearsed fragility. "I don't know what I did to provoke it, Eddy. I was just passing the hall, and she appeared, wild-eyed."

Lucy edged closer, the frame of the doorway cutting the scene into slices. Josephine stood by the counter, her hair a little mussed but her eyes bright, alive with performance. She held out her arm.

The gash was fresh, a thin line of blood trailing down her skin. Not deep enough to warrant fear. Deliberate.

"She smashed a glass," Josephine whispered, her lips trembling in mock restraint. "Then she... she cut me."

Ed stood opposite her, barefoot, hair tousled from sleep. His face was grey with exhaustion, his jaw set. He looked at the blood, at Josephine's shaking hand, then away. His fingers flexed at his sides, restless, as though he were searching for a verdict that wouldn't exist.

"Christ, Josie..." His voice was heavy with fatigue and his

hangover. But edged with concern. *He believes her already,* Lucy thought. *It ends in blood. Is this the end, then? Is this her final play?*

Josephine's voice broke with practiced fragility. "She's not safe, Eddy. She's a danger to herself, Or you. And me."

Lucy's mouth went dry. She clutched the doorframe until her knuckles ached.

Ed rubbed his forehead, the gesture of a man drowning in memory and responsibility. "I'll... God, I'll deal with it later. I need to shower. I've got court today."

He will not participate, Lucy thought, hating him, loving him. *Even with somebody physically injured in his home, he won't acknowledge it. He won't accept it. He's worse than his father. Who did I marry?*

Josephine took a moment as though deciding on the best course of action, the best tactic.

"No," she pleaded, stepping closer, eyes wide and glistening. "You need to see it now. Before it gets worse. She's unravelling. I'm scared." She pressed her cut into his line of sight, wincing prettily. "You don't understand what it's like. Hearing her muttering outside my door at night, hearing the stairs creak and not knowing if it's her—"

"She wasn't," Ed started, but his voice faltered. He pinched the bridge of his nose. The strain made him look older, his body bowing under the invisible weight of both his sister's pain and his wife's supposed instability.

Josephine lowered her gaze, then looked back up with devastating softness. "You've always protected me, Ed. You're all I've got. If you don't believe me, if you don't help me, I don't know what I'll do."

The injustice roared up inside Lucy. Her body moved without permission.

"That's a lie!" she shouted, stepping into the hall.

Ed turned sharply. Josephine gasped, clutching her arm to her chest like a cornered saint.

"She did that to herself!" Lucy cried, her voice shaking with fury. "She staged all of this!"

"Lucy, please!" Josephine's words sounded like a knife sheathed in velvet. "You're not well."

Lucy's throat burned. "Don't you dare! That cut is shallow and you know it. You pressed the glass into your own arm." She pointed to the kitchen. "And that blood? It's smeared on the counter, not spattered. You *painted* it here."

Josephine huffed and began to walk. Lucy turned and went with her, and Ed trailed behind.

In the kitchen, Ed's eyes flicked between them, confusion clouded with fatigue. He did not want to be there. *He'd let us tear each other apart if it meant he didn't have to make a bloody decision.* He ran his hand down his face as though wishing he could scrub the whole scene from existence.

"Look at me, Ed," Lucy begged. "You *know* me. You know I wouldn't do this."

"Stop." His voice was sharp, final.

Lucy's world trembled.

"I don't know what to think anymore," Ed said, his shoulders sagging. He turned his gaze to Josephine's arm again, then back to Lucy, trapped between blood and doubt. "But this… this isn't normal." His voice broke slightly on the last word.

She reached for him. "Ed."

He stepped back. "You need professional help."

The sentence cracked over her like a whip. Professional help. The tone final, damning, the words of a man ready to sign papers.

Josephine lowered her gaze with exquisite timing, tears brimming. She dabbed the wound again, biting her lip like a child.

Ed's voice softened, but the words still killed. "I can't keep living like this. It's tearing me apart."

Lucy staggered back, glass biting her heels. She felt the wet stinging pain only distantly. "You believe her," she whispered.

Ed didn't answer. His silence was worse. He turned and left the room, his footsteps heavy.

Josephine's lips curled the moment he disappeared. The smallest of smiles which were quick, sharp, and aimed only at Lucy. Then she dabbed delicately at her wound once more, the picture of injured innocence.

Rage, grief, and fear swirled into something cold and sharp.

The trap had been sprung.

She rushed after Ed and followed him upstairs, her pulse roaring in her ears. The house seemed to press in on her with every step, its walls tight with accusation. The bedroom was warm from the radiator but felt cold all the same. His office suit lay draped over the bed; he stood in front of the mirror, tying his tie with jerky, impatient movements.

"Ed," Lucy said, breathless.

He didn't look at her. "Not now."

"Yes, now." She caught his arm, forcing him to turn. "She cut herself. You saw how shallow it was. You know she staged it. Please, Ed – please tell me you can see that. I know you've been through a lot. I know she's suffered. I know *you've* suffered. But I have to believe we have something here."

His face contorted, torn between anger and weariness. His eyes were rimmed red, like he hadn't slept in days. "I don't know what to believe anymore, Lucy!" His voice cracked, filling the room with its rawness.

"You believe her over me?"

The question came out raw and, Lucy knew, ridiculous. It was the question of a woman desperate to believe there was still a way out. It was the question of a woman who should've known better.

"I believe something's wrong." His hands shook as he yanked the tie knot into place. "With you. With all of this. It's spiralling out of control. *That's* what I believe."

Her breath came shallow. "You can't mean that. You know what she is, Ed. My brakes didn't cut themselves. She tried to kill me... and that's not even mentioning everything else. If you loved me, you'd at least *try* to see where I'm coming from."

He slammed the wardrobe door shut, startling her. "Even the neighbours are worried! They told me they've heard you ranting, raving in the garden at night. Shouting at shadows. Do you have any idea how humiliating that is?"

Lucy reeled. "The neighbours? What are you talking about? I've never—"

"They've *heard* it," Ed snapped. "They asked me if you're unwell." He looked away as though the shame was too heavy to face her.

Lucy shook her head, horror creeping in. "That's her. She's spreading lies to them, just like she's doing to you. She's turning the whole world against me."

Ed grabbed his jacket, his movements harsh. "No, Lucy. You're turning the world against yourself."

"Ed," Her voice broke. She grabbed his hand, clinging to him. "It's her. She's dangerous. If you'd just open your eyes."

He ripped his hand away, eyes wild with exhaustion. "I can't keep doing this!" His face flushed with fury. "Every day is another accusation, another scene. I come home to chaos. I wake up to chaos. I work too damn hard to have to deal with this! I deserve a wife, Luce, a wife, not a... a project."

For a moment, he faltered. His breath stuttered. His shoulders dropped as though some hidden truth pressed down. Lucy thought she saw the boy he once was; the protector, the brother, the killer. His lips trembled, but instead of confessing, he swallowed it all back down.

Tears burned Lucy's eyes. "The truth is in front of you. She's manipulating you, manipulating all of us. She staged that cut, just like she staged the nursery, the diary, the car. Please, Ed. Please."

But Ed's gaze slid away. He moved toward the door, his breathing ragged. "Get some help, Lucy. Before it's too late."

The words struck harder than a slap.

"Ed, don't leave me with her," she whispered, but the plea barely left her lips before the door slammed shut, the sound rattling through her bones.

The silence left behind was deafening.

Lucy pressed her palms to the dresser, leaning hard, her reflection staring back, pale, frantic, hollow-eyed. She saw exactly what Josephine wanted Ed to see: a woman unravelled, a wife losing her grip.

Her knees buckled. For a moment she thought she might sink to the floor and never rise again.

But something else stirred beneath the despair. Cold. Clear.

She whispered into the wood: "No. I am not mad. I won't let her win."

The words steadied her breath. Slowly, she lifted her head, meeting her own reflection. Not broken. Not yet.

Josephine had Ed. She had the neighbours. She had his parents.

But Lucy had herself. And Charlotte.

She straightened, wiped her face with trembling hands, and grabbed her bag. Phone. Keys. Coat. Every movement deliberate, ritualistic.

As she closed the bedroom door behind her, the house seemed to lean in, listening, amused. She ignored it. *I am done with this house which always seems way too bloody alive.* She felt like punching a wall just to hurt the damned thing.

On the stairs, her footsteps were steady. At the front door, her hand didn't falter. She pulled it open, the bracing air biting her cheeks and stepped outside.

The cold slapped clarity into her.

She would go to Charlotte, like she had done before. Only this time, Lucy would listen to her friend. She would let her help. She wouldn't bury her head in the sand any longer.

Because if she didn't act soon, Josephine would take everything and destroy her completely.

26

December 12th

Lucy drove with her knuckles white around the steering wheel, the car heater blowing stale air that only seemed to dry her throat further. The road blurred past in streaks of pale wintery sun, her eyes burning from too many tears. Ed's voice still rang in her head: *"You need professional help."* And Josephine's smile, that faint curl of triumph in the corner of her mouth, branded her thoughts.

By the time she pulled up outside Charlotte's house, her chest felt hollow, her whole body buzzing with nervous exhaustion. When Lucy knocked with a tremoring hand and Charlotte opened the door, the world immediately softened.

Charlotte pulled her into a hug before Lucy could even speak. "You look like you've run through a storm," she murmured against Lucy's hair.

Lucy crumpled into the embrace, her chest heaving. The tears came again, raw and hot. "I can't, Charlotte, I can't do this anymore. She's winning. He believes her. About everything. I know you've tried to help. To give advice. But I've been... nothing."

"Luce, hush," Charlotte whispered.

"I've done nothing and *been* nothing. I *am* nothing."

"Quiet, hon. Come inside."

Charlotte pulled her into the hallway then shut the door. She guided her to the sofa, pressed a tissue into her hand, and poured tea into a mug that was chipped but beloved. She sat close, legs crossed, her gaze steady and kind.

"Take it slow," Charlotte said. "What's happened now?"

She wants to know if this could possibly get crazier, Lucy thought, dabbing her cheeks. *Well, buckle up.*

Lucy told her. The blood on the counter, the shards of glass, Josephine's self-inflicted wound. Ed's refusal to listen, his words about the neighbours. She withheld the revelation about Ed killing Josephine's rapist when he was younger. Whatever else was true, that man, *that stranger,* was still her husband.

She spoke in a rush, her hands shaking, her voice climbing higher as she relived it. When she finished, she sat trembling, waiting for disbelief, waiting for Charlotte to ask if she'd imagined it all.

But Charlotte only exhaled through her nose, slow and measured, and set her tea down carefully. "I believe you."

Lucy's head jerked up. "You do?"

"Of course I do." Charlotte's eyes flashed with certainty. "How could you even ask me that? I know you. You're not mad, Lucy. You're exhausted, battered from being cornered in your own home, but you are not what she's trying to make you."

Lucy pressed her fingers to her lips, overwhelmed. The relief at being believed threatened to undo her completely.

Charlotte leaned forward, her voice low but firm. "Listen to me. Josephine is clever. Ruthless. She's manipulating Ed's guilt, twisting his love for her into something poisonous. But that doesn't mean you've lost him."

"He doesn't look at me the same anymore," Lucy whispered.

"He doesn't look at *himself* the same. I bet," Charlotte countered. "But you and Edward, I'm sure you can be happy again. You just need to take her out of the picture once and for all."

Lucy stared at her friend, her body thrumming with anxious energy. "But how? She's in everything. She's turned his parents, his colleagues, even the neighbours, everyone is against me."

Charlotte reached across, gripping Lucy's trembling hands in both of hers. Her grip was warm, steadying. "You are stronger than she is. Stronger than you realise. You've held yourself together through lies, gaslighting, humiliation. That takes strength. And you're clever too. You know how to fight this. Not by screaming, not by proving yourself over and over. By showing Edward the truth in a way Josephine can't twist."

Lucy blinked, tears brimming again. "I tried that, Char. I had a recording. I told him about the photo of me she'd scratched the bloody face off. I can't show him if he doesn't want to see."

"Then you try again," Charlotte said simply. "Because you're not a woman who lies down and lets someone else write her ending. You never have been."

Lucy swallowed hard, staring down at their joined hands. Somewhere outside, a bus rumbled past. Ordinary sounds, grounding her.

Charlotte squeezed tighter. "You've survived this long, Luce. You're a capable woman, more than capable. Now stop letting her define you. Remove her. However, you need to. Then rebuild with Edward, piece by piece."

For the first time in weeks, a flicker of something close to hope stirred in Lucy's chest. It was faint, fragile, but it was there.

She nodded, almost to herself. "Remove her."

Charlotte's mouth curved into a grim smile. "Exactly. Take back what's yours. And when she's gone, you'll see. I'm sure the two of you can be happy again. I know it."

Lucy leaned back into the sofa, letting the warmth of Charlotte's house wrap around her like armour. In that moment, she knew Charlotte was right: Josephine had to go.

That evening, the street was blue with a layer of ice. Lucy let the car door thud shut and stood a moment, keys cold in her palm, listening to the kind of quiet that makes the world seem sane and reasonable and civilised. Her breath ghosted out and was taken at once by the night.

Charlotte's words were still warm her chest. *Remove her; take back what's yours.* An entire day at school had done nothing to quieten them.

Inside, the hall lamp had been left on. No voices. No music. No Josephine humming her nameless tune. Ed's coat peg was empty.

"Ed?" The name sounded almost polite. Too formal. *I was never supposed to say my husband's name in this tone here,* a distant part of her noted. *It was never supposed to be like this.*

She stood in the hall and felt the ache under her sternum. Sleep would be a kindness. But the marriage bed upstairs felt booby-trapped. Still, she could collapse, she could forget, for a little while.

She pushed open the bedroom door, then stopped as a gasp escaped her.

A mobile turned above the bed. Their bed. Not the cot. *Our marital bloody bed.*

She had to blink to be sure of movement, but there it was: tiny moons and stars, moving with hypnotic rhythm.

On the bed, on their bed lay the doll. It had been tucked in with a shirt of Ed's. Grey-blue, collar frayed, a missing button Lucy had meant to replace the first month they lived here, the one he still wore, the one they joked about. The plastic eyelids were half closed in that wrong way dolls have of imitating sleep.

On the wall above the bed, in a handwriting Lucy already knew in her bones, a message had been written in black marker. The loops were too deliberate, the tail on the *y* like a flourish. *Our family.*

For a long time, she simply stood there and let the scene compose itself with terrible patience. The nursery had been a test. This was the real deal. *She's violated our bedroom.*

Terror tried to make Lucy run. This was like something out of a horror film. Josephine might do anything. Might do to Lucy what she'd done to Becca. Might go further, succeed where she'd failed before.

The mobile turned. Lucy stepped closer to the bed and looked down at the plastic face. It had been powdered. Someone had taken a soft brush and blushed its cheeks in a parody of life. She reached for the shirt almost without meaning to, pinched the seam and felt the ghost of Ed's body in the fabric.

The words on the wall sat there, smug as a stamp: *Our family*. She had seen Josephine's lists in the kitchen, and the particular slanting *r*, the way she is dotting her *i* as if she expected applause. There was no need to compare, no need to pretend anyone else might have written this.

She turned toward the door to leave, to fetch her phone, to gather the evidence Charlotte would want her to gather, and the door moved of its own accord an inch, then two, then slammed shut.

The sound made the mobile swing hard once, then it found its pace again. Lucy stood very still and felt the grip of adrenaline go to all the places in her body that still believed fighting was worth it. She rushed to the door and threw it open.

Josephine rushed in, causing Lucy to back away as if from wild animal. She shut the door behind her then stood with her back to it, one hand behind her, as if she wanted to be immediately aware if somebody tried to interrupt them.

"Hello," she said, as if Lucy had arrived late to a small, intimate party.

Lucy did not answer. She did not trust her voice.

"You scared the mobile." Josephine tilted her head and watched the moons and stars shift. "It likes to be watched. Most things do."

"You need to let me leave," Lucy said.

"I thought you wanted to stay?"

"This r-room," Lucy stuttered. "You need to let me leave this room."

"Do you like it?" she asked. "It's better now, don't you think? Our baby didn't like the cot. Our baby wanted a special place. A place that smelled like Daddy."

Lucy's throat shifted like she might scream. The word *Daddy* cut through her with a sickening sharpness that left her ragged. "Josephine," she said very slowly. "You know that's just a doll, right?"

How out of it is she? Lucy screamed in her head. *End her, Lucy. This is it. She's boxed you in. Won't let you leave. It's self-defence.*

But Lucy couldn't spring into action like she wanted. Her limbs refused to obey.

"Oh, darling." Josephine's mouth made a shape that could have been pity if it hadn't been theatre. "It's not *just* a doll. When it comes to me and Eddy, nothing is *just* anything."

She drifted closer to the bed and, with two fingertips, smoothed the shirt over the doll's chest, restoring the crease to the special way she liked it, apparently. The fingers lingered, stroking the plastic curve of the forehead with a softness that made Lucy want to peel off her skin.

"He wore this the day he fixed my bike," Josephine murmured, to the doll or the room, but not to Lucy. Lucy knew that somehow; these words weren't meant for her. "I fell off because the chain snapped and he ran, like in films, and picked me up and carried me home. He always carried me home." She looked up at last and held Lucy's eyes. "Don't you see? It was always supposed to be me and him."

"This is an adult's shirt," Lucy said softly, as if this psycho would ever hear reason. "I don't think he wore this as a child, Josie."

Again, she'd used *Josie*. As if she could help her. As if she didn't hate her.

Make a run for it, Lucy scolded herself. *Go. Now.*

"You don't understand," Josephine went on, voice lowering. "You never will." She began to move again, a slow orbit that made Lucy must turn to keep her in view or else be flanked. "That's why we walked away together by the water, and I held his hand, and I told him he was a hero." Her smile had become a relic. "That's why I had to frighten Becca."

The way she said *frighten* was so sharp it almost squeaked.

Lucy was breathing like a person who had read bad instructions on how to inhale and exhale. "You didn't just *frighten* her. You put her in hospital."

Josephine considered, as if consulting her own archive of the event, her own messed-up version. "Hospitals are just buildings." She took another small step and the distance between them became exactly wrong. "You keep confusing what things are called with what they are."

That doesn't mean anything, Lucy wanted to snap. *Except one thing: you're too far gone.*

She reached down and stroked the doll's cheek with the back

of her hand in a gesture that would have been tenderness if it had been a real child. "We didn't scream when we put him in the river," she said conversationally. "We were so quiet. That's how you know you're doing something important. Your body becomes a room where you don't want to slam the door."

Lucy swallowed. The mobile turned. The marker on the wall glared.

"And now," Josephine said, brightening as if arriving at the solution in a puzzle book, "you're the one in the way."

The temperature dropped Lucy stepped back, but there was nowhere to go that wasn't in Josephine's path.

Josephine looked at the doll's face again. "I lost a baby once," she said. No performative tremor now. The words were delivered flat and emotionless. "I won't lose another."

In Lucy's head, she heard Susan's voice: *Thankfully, she had a miscarriage.*

"Step aside," Lucy said. *Not like that. Put some steel into it.* "Step aside, Josie. Now."

Josephine moved just enough to indulge the idea. "Why," she asked softly, as if she were reciting a line in a play, "would I ever make it easy for you?"

Lucy's eyes went to the marker. Evidence. Charlotte's voice, practical, in her head: *Show him the truth in a way she can't twist.* She thought of taking a photograph. She thought of the door behind Josephine, closed, imagined what Josephine would do if Lucy darted for it.

Josephine tilted her head like a bird. "It's sweet," she said, almost kindly, "that you still think *he* is the person to convince. He was ours before he was yours. Blood is thicker, as they say..." She considered the mobile, put out a finger, stopped it, then released it so it spun again.

That's why she does to me. Stops me. Lets me spin. Stops me again.

"You aren't listening, Lucy. I've been doing you a favour. Setting the terms. Teaching you how to leave... giving you an excuse. Me. You can end this farce of a marriage and blame your sweet sister-in-law. I'm doing you a *kindness.*"

"I live here," Lucy said, the words she'd stated so many times, over and over until even she was beginning to get tired of them.

Josephine's eyes shone. "So does our future." She nodded at the doll, snug in the old shirt. "Our family." The two words spread like damp.

"Say it plainly," Lucy said. Her own voice surprised her again, low and even, the kind of voice children obey because they don't want to disappoint. "You've threatened me more than once. You're threatening me now. What exactly are you telling me you will do?"

Josephine took one thoughtful step closer. Up this close the pupils of her eyes looked too wide for the light.

"Finish what I started," Josephine said.

"Step aside," Lucy said again. "Or I'll call the police and you can tell them all about how you forced your brother to kill a boy who may or may not have raped you."

Josephine's smile held. "Ah, so you think you can slander *my* credibility," she muttered. "Ed's very worried about... who is it, Luce? Me or you? Ah, that's right." She snapped her fingers. "And it's not just Eddy. The neighbours too. You've been so loud, darling. All that shouting at shadows." She leaned in one breath further. "But call them if you like. I'll hold the baby while we wait. The commotion might upset the little one."

When Lucy spoke again her mouth was dry. "Move," she said quietly, "or I scream. And this time the neighbours will hear something real."

A calculation crossed Josephine's face. On someone else it would have looked like reconsideration. On her, it looked like a sadist deciding to let a street cat writhe for a few minutes longer before finishing the job. She stepped half a pace sideways, not enough to fully clear the way. Just enough.

"Good girl," Josephine said.

This is your moment, Lucy thought in Charlotte's voice. *This is your chance. Do something, Luce. Do it now.*

Lucy didn't run for the door. Instead, she took her phone from her pocket without looking down and, keeping her eyes on Josephine's, lifted it. One click. The soft sound of a photograph. Then another. The message on the wall and the mobile and the doll in the shirt and Josephine in the same frame, smiling, because she seemingly couldn't wipe away that plastic smile.

"Evidence?" Josephine said with a yawn. "Little trophies meant to inspire... fear? Loyalty? I keep mine in a box. You prefer the Cloud." She reached out, and for one terrible moment Lucy thought she would take the phone from her hand like you take a toy from a child. Instead, she smoothed the air between them, not touching. "Don't be silly enough to sleep here," she advised.

Lucy didn't run. She left the bedroom and only then let herself breathe with the heavy panic that had gripped her bones.

Lucy felt the tremor begin in her hands and move up her arms like storm. She pressed her back to the wall and let the plaster ground here. She was alive. For now and she was determined to stand her ground.

27

December 13th

She couldn't sleep. She tossed and turned. The air itself felt unsettled, the walls whispering that something was moving within them. And then she heard it, a sound so out of place, so chilling, she thought at first, she had imagined it.

A lullaby.

Faint, tuneless, but steady.

She crept onto the landing. The spare-room door glowed faintly, lamplight bleeding out into the darkness. It was ajar by only an inch, as if the room were trying to tempt her inside.

Her hand trembled as she pushed it open.

Josephine was in the chair by a cot. It didn't look like the one from the nursery. This was newer, a dark green colour. *She's built her own cot. For her child. The one she wants to raise with her brother.* Each sentence fell surreally in Lucy's mind.

Her figure was half-lit by the lamp. Her hair had come loose, red strands clinging damply to her cheeks, as though she had sweated through some unseen exertion. Assembling the cot? In her arms she held the doll, wrapped in Ed's old shirt, and rocked it with deliberate rhythm.

"Sleep tight, little one," Josephine whispered, her voice frayed, raw. "Mummy's here. Mummy's here now."

The words crawled under Lucy's skin, making her throat tighten. The mobile above the crib spun wildly, moons and stars flickering across the walls like restless shadows. Lucy knew if she ever made it through this, if she ever became a mother, she wouldn't get them a mobile of moon and stars.

Lucy stepped further inside. "Stop it," she said, her voice barely audible as fear tried to take her tongue.

Josephine didn't react. She pressed her lips to the doll's forehead, humming off-key, her body swaying with devotion.

"I said *stop it!*" Lucy's voice rose.

Josephine's head snapped up. Her eyes gleamed with something feral. She rose so abruptly the chair skidded against the wall. The doll slipped from her arms, rolling onto the bed.

"You stole him from me!" she shrieked. For several seconds, the world slowed. Lucy saw Josephine as she truly was. The mask had slipped. Her madness had frayed her mental defences down to a stub.

Lucy experienced a small moment of petty victory. Lucy knew, without a single doubt, she wasn't insane. Her sister-in-law was.

And then Josephine lunged.

The force of her body slammed Lucy back against the wall, knocking the breath from her lungs. Her skull rattled against the plaster, pain flaring white behind her eyes. A picture frame above them shook loose and fell, shattering on the carpet.

Josephine's nails raked down her cheek, fire branding her skin. "He was always mine!" she screamed, spittle flecking her lips. "Always!"

Lucy shoved at her shoulders, but Josephine was strong, stronger than her thin frame suggested. Lucy felt her hair wrenched, her head yanked sideways, her balance nearly gone.

"You think you're the wife, the saviour?" Josephine snarled. Her forehead pressed against Lucy's, breath sour with wine. "You're nothing. Nothing compared to me."

Lucy twisted, trying to free herself. "You're sick!" she gasped, her voice strangled by Josephine's weight.

Josephine's eyes glittered with madness. "Do you know why he saved me? Why he's always been mine?" She ground the words against Lucy's ear. "Because I carried *his child* once. Did he tell you? Did he?"

Lucy froze, her chest clenching as if her heart had missed a beat.

Josephine laughed, high and jagged, almost joyous. "After the rape, I was pregnant. And then I lost it. But it was mine. It was *ours.* That bound us. Not vows. Not rings. *Blood!*"

Lucy's horror transformed into rage. She shoved with every ounce of strength left in her. Josephine stumbled backward, nearly tripping over the chair.

"He's not yours!" Lucy shouted, voice breaking.

Josephine bared her teeth, lunging again. They grappled, crashing into the cot. The wood groaned under the impact. The doll tumbled out, hitting the floor with a sickening crack. Its head snapped off, rolling slowly across the carpet until it rested against the skirting board, eyes staring glassily at nothing.

Josephine's scream ripped through the house, raw and animal. "No! Not again!" Her voice shredded with grief and fury. She dropped to her knees, clutching the doll's headless body, rocking it for a moment as if willing it back to life. Then, as though something in her had broken cleanly, she whirled on Lucy with pure hatred.

Her hand darted to the shards of glass glittering on the floor from the shattered picture frame. Blood welled instantly in her palm as she gripped one. She rose, eyes blazing, brandishing the shard like a knife.

"You ruined everything!" she howled. "And now I'll ruin your pretty little face. And your pretty little womb. *You* won't be Mummy! You *can't.*"

Lucy stumbled back, hands raised, her breath coming in ragged gasps. Josephine's face was carved in shadow and fury, a grotesque mask. The hot edge of a glass shard bit into Lucy's face, blood weeping like tears.

The door burst open.

"Josie!" Ed's voice.

He stood frozen in the hall, rain dripping from his hair, his suit rumpled as though he had run through the storm. It was only then that she heard it. The lightning outside. The thunder. The hammering rain. A backdrop to this madness which had become quiet because it was so loud in here.

His face drained of colour as his eyes registered the scene: Lucy, her cheek bleeding, chest heaving; Josephine, blood on her hand, a shard of glass raised high; the cot cracked, the doll decapitated on the floor.

For the first time, there was no room for excuses. No performance could mask what Josephine had become.

And Edward could only stand there, horror rooting him to the spot, as the storm howled its approval outside.

His lips parted, but no sound came. He looked between the women, his gaze torn in two: Lucy's flushed face, eyes wild with terror, and Josephine, her hair matted, blood streaming from her palm, the shard of glass trembling in her grip.

"Ed," Lucy gasped, her voice raw. "Help me."

Josephine was quicker. She dropped the shard into the cot with a clatter and stretched her bleeding hand toward him. "Ed," she whispered, her tone sweet as sugar melting on the tongue. "She tried to kill me. Again. She's out of control."

The words hung in the storm-filled air, absurd and yet weighted by weeks of poison already planted.

Lucy shook her head violently. "No – no, you saw it! You *had* to see it. She was going to—" She pointed at the cot, at the doll's broken head lying on the carpet like mute testimony. "She's been playing a sick game in our house. When I confronted her, she lunged at me. You know she's capable of this, Ed!"

Ed swayed where he stood, his expression fractured. "What... what is happening here?" He spoke his like father: like a man who wanted to close his eyes and wake elsewhere.

Josephine stumbled forward, pressing her body against his chest, smearing blood down his shirt. She clung to him, her voice shaking, pitched perfectly. "She hates me. She's jealous. I woke up and she attacked me. Look—" She lifted her cut hand as though it were a holy wound. "She's unravelled, Ed. She needs help. I tried, but..."

"Stop it!" Lucy shouted, her voice cracking into a sob. "Don't you dare twist this again. You can't talk your way out of this one."

The storm punctuated her words with another crash, the window rattling in its frame. The mobile above the crib spun drunkenly, moons and stars colliding, a parody of harmony.

Ed's eyes darting back to Lucy. For a heartbeat, she saw it, the flicker of belief, the recognition of truth. His lips parted, breath shallow.

But Josephine's arms circled tighter around him, her head tucked against his shoulder like a child's. Her voice was muffled, broken. "You promised you'd always protect me."

Lucy's gut tightened. She knew, without a doubt, there was nothing she could say to compete with that. These were promises forged long before Lucy had ever entered their lives. These were deep roots, and Lucy was a weed.

Ed didn't answer. His silence said everything.

Lucy took a shaking step back. The room pressed in on her, thick with dust, blood, the ghost of Josephine's lullaby. She realised with bone-deep certainty that she was standing at the edge of something that could not be undone. Either Josephine left the house, or she would.

"Look at me, Ed," Lucy pleaded. Her voice had thinned to a desperate thread. "This is your choice. Right now. Do you see her for what she is, or do you stay blind?"

Josephine lifted her face, her eyes glistening with unshed tears. She pressed her cheek to Ed's chest, her lips curving in the faintest smile that Lucy alone could see.

"Well?" Lucy demanded.

Ed tenderly stroked his hand through Josephine's hair, more affection in the movement than he'd ever shown her. "She's a special girl, Luce. You can't treat her this way. She needs delicacy. She needs soft, gentle love."

Lucy froze as Josephine's voice dropped to a whisper, cruel and deliberate. "I carried his child once. Did he tell you that?" Her smile was venomous, triumphant. "After the rape. I was pregnant. I lost it. But it was ours, Lucy. Mine and his. That bound us forever."

The words didn't enter her like a knife. Knives are clean. They seeped, oily and cold, and coated her ribs from the inside. Bile rising in her throat. Josephine with a swelling no one saw, a secret beating like a fist in the dark, Ed's hand offered to a grief he would never name. She tasted metal as she waited for her husband to deny this.

"It wasn't... his?"

"My rapist's?" Josephine tutted and shook her head. "Nah-uh. It was Eddy's."

This can't be happening, Lucy thought, but it was. Ed had gone dead-eyed, stroking his little sister's hair, refusing to look at Lucy anymore.

"You're sick," Lucy whispered, her voice breaking. "You're sick and twisted and—"

Josephine laughed, a jagged, high-pitched sound that grated against the thunder. "That's why Becca had to go. She thought she could have him. But I showed her. And now it's your turn."

"Josie," Ed whispered, but it wasn't a reprimand, not even a stern warning. It was the tone a powerful man used with his favourite pet.

"He won't stop me." Josephine disentangled herself from her brother's embrace and then knelt, picking up another shard of glass. "He knows what has to happen."

He's just standing there, Lucy thought, very slowly, as Ed watched and Josephine took a step toward her.

Josephine lunged with a guttural scream.

Lucy backed out of the room, head pounding, adrenaline and terror and a sickness so deep, she knew she'd never feel clean again. Josephine chased her, mouth open in a primal cry.

The world tilted beneath her, the edge of the banister digging into her back. Lucy's hands scrabbled for purchase, her vision narrowing with panic. The landing light stuttered as if the storm were breathing through it. The gloss on the handrail was slick under her palm.

Josephine's nails tore at her skin, her eyes blazing with feral determination. Somewhere behind them Ed's breath heaved fast, frightened, a sound she had never heard in him. He reached, as if to intervene, then hesitated, and the hesitation burned.

Is he afraid for her? Or for me?

"You don't belong here!" Josephine screamed, shaking her. Lucy's teeth gnashed together, and she bit the end of her tongue. "He's mine!" Spit flecked Lucy's cheek.

Something broke inside Lucy. Not a snap. A relief of tension. A rope coming loose. The weeks of torment, the lies, the gaslighting, the violence, the blood. All of it surged into a single, blinding moment of clarity.

She wasn't mad. She wasn't imagining it. Josephine wanted her gone and had wanted her gone the moment she was released from prison, and if Lucy didn't act now, she would be.

"Get—off—me," Lucy said, teeth bared, the words ground out, low and animal. She planted her feet, felt for the runner's seam with the balls of her toes, found the plank beneath. Her left hand slid off Josephine's wrist, dropped, and then she drove both palms hard into the cap of Josephine's shoulder.

With a cry torn from the deepest part of her, Lucy shoved.

For a split-second Josephine's expression flickered from rage to shock. Then her heel slipped on the polished wood.

Time slowed.

Ed's scream tore through the landing. "Josie!"

Josephine's hands clawed at the air, grasping for something to hold. Her fingers raked Lucy's collarbone; Lucy flinched, but there was nothing left to grip. Josephine slammed against the banister; the wood groaned; the finial shuddered on its post. The top newel creaked. Not a break, a protest. Then she toppled forward.

The first thud at the top step sounded like a trunk dropped by a careless mover. Then the repeated, awful percussion: shoulder, hip, skull against tread, a dull drum that counted out the steps with brutal precision. Her scream cut off and then began again in two short, ripped sounds. Then came only the sick rhythm of falling, punctuated by the sharp crack of bone on the lip of a stair, the slap of skin, followed by the scrape of fabric. Halfway down her ankle twisted under her and her body turned so she went the rest of the way sideways, rolled by the geometry of pain.

Lucy stood frozen, her chest heaving, the world spinning. The storm's roar filled the silence Josephine left behind. The house seemed to inhale and not exhale. For one dizzy, wrong second, the hallway at the bottom looked like a stage set from a play where someone had misjudged a stunt.

At the bottom of the stairs, Josephine's body lay crumpled and still, blood pooling beneath her head, seeping into the fibres of the carpet. One hand had come to rest palm up, showing the cut from the shard of glass. Her hair spilled like blood-tinged seaweed across the tile.

"Josie, my Josie!" Edward rushed past Lucy, almost knocking her aside as he hurtled down the stairs. He dropped to his knees, pulling Josephine into his arms, his sobs ragged and unrestrained. "No, no, no..." He cupped the back of her head, then flinched at the warmth on his palm, at the slickness he found there.

Lucy gripped the banister, her hands slick with blood from the fight. She looked down at them in horror at the red blood, sticky and glistening in the dim light. It clothed her fingers, got into the fibre of her skin. She had the absurd thought that she would never again be able to open her phone with her thumbprint; she had become someone else.

"Stay with me," Ed said into Josephine's hair, rocking her, that old childhood rhythm he must have used long before Lucy ever knew him. "Please, God, Jo, stay with me." His voice shifted, softer, a register Lucy had never heard him use. He said her name as if it were the last thing he would ever speak: "Jo."

I have just killed a woman.

Lucy stood there in shock. She couldn't move. She pressed the inside of her wrist to her mouth to keep down the bile.

"Call an ambulance!" E's head snapped up, his voice breaking.

Lucy fumbled for her phone, her fingers slippery. The screen smeared under her touch; she wiped it on her pyjama bottoms and punched at the screen. Her voice when it came was thin and high. She gave the address clearly, automatic in her teacher voice. They asked about breathing; Lucy looked and saw the small, irregular movement of Josephine's chest, how it caught and stuttered. "Yes," she said. "Yes. She's breathing. There's blood. Head. Uh, she hit her head. Sorry. Fell." Lucy paused, tried to speak clearly. "She fell down the stairs." The operator's voice was a rope; Lucy held it with both hands until they said help was on the way.

She ended the call and leaned forward over the stairhead. "They're coming," she said.

Ed didn't answer. His forehead was pressed to Josephine's temple, lips moving. Prayer, plea, apology. The words weren't for Lucy. His hands were clumsy with tenderness; he tried to staunch the bleeding with his cuff and then, realising what he was doing, stripped off his shirt with awkward fury and pressed it to the wound. He looked up, not at Lucy, but at the family photographs on the opposite wall, as if asking them to justify themselves.

She's not dead, Lucy thought, staring. *I might not be a killer yet. Calm. Breathe.*

From somewhere far away, sirens began. An impossibly short time later – some part of her was aware time had fragmented and was doing funny things – blue light swept the ceiling in bars; for a second the house looked underwater.

Paramedics burst in, boots pounding, carrying equipment that rattled with urgency. One went to his knees so fast Lucy thought he would hurt himself. The other swept a glance over the scene the way good teachers count heads. "Head trauma," he said to the air, already gloving up. "Possible skull fracture. GCS… unresponsive to verbal. Sir, I need you to step back."

Ed clung for a second longer and then let his sister's head

down as if returning something sacred to an altar. He stumbled backward and hit the wall with a soft thud. He folded his hands as if had remembered a prayer he hadn't used yet.

"Ma'am, are you injured?" The second paramedic had turned to Lucy without taking his eyes off his Josephine. She shook her head, then nodded, then shook it again. He took in the smear on her face, the claw tracks. "Are your injuries urgent?"

Lucy somehow shook her head, and he returned his focus to Josephine.

"We're going to move you, all right, love?" He spoke to the unconscious body as if she could hear.

They slid the stretcher, fastened the straps with clicks that sounded like decisions. *Do I want her to die?* Lucy thought distantly. *Would that be better for everyone?*

The collar went on, white and uncompromising. "On three," the lead said, and the three of them (Ed had stepped forward without permission and the paramedic didn't have the spare hand to stop him) lifted. Josephine's arm flopped out and then was caught and tucked onto the stretcher.

"She's alive," one paramedic said, already fastening straps. "Unconscious, but alive. We need to move now."

"Which hospital?" Ed's voice cracked. The paramedic told him; the name landed like a foreign city

Ed followed, clutching her hand, whispering words Lucy couldn't hear. His lips moved. *I've got you. I'm here. Don't leave me.* Words Lucy had wanted applied to her and never would now. His bare chest had gooseflesh; a red smear crossed his ribs like war paint. He bent his head and kept up his love-filled whispers as they stepped into the night.

He didn't look back at her.

Not once.

The blue light strobed the hallway; neighbours' faces

ghosted and disappeared at the edge of vision like white moths. The ambulance doors slammed. The siren wound itself up again and the sound moved away, stretched to a thread and then cut.

And in that silence, heavier than blame, Lucy understood what had broken could never be put back together.

Lucy sat for a long time on the top step, her hand pressed against her cheek, the blood sticky and stiffening.

When she finally stood, her knees objected with a *pop* that was like a gun going off. She went down three steps and stopped, not trusting the stairs any more than they trusted her. On the bannister was a faint smear where Josephine had hit shone under the landing light. Lucy reached out and wiped it with the edge of her sleeve. The fabric darkened. It would never quite come clean.

Unsure of what else to do, she rang Charlotte. Her voice came out as a staccato shudder as she explained what had happened.

"Are you hurt?" Charlotte asked.

"No. I don't think so."

For now, Lucy thought grimly.

"You sound like you're in shock, hon."

"I'm going to the hospital," Lucy said with more certainty.

"I'm driving back right no—"

"You've tried to be there for me," Lucy said. "You've tried to help. But I kept coming back here. I kept thinking I could win. Now, look at me. Look what's happened."

"This is *not* your fault, Luce. She pushed you to it."

"It is. That's what they are all going to think." Lucy said dully, then hung up.

Lucy looked down the staircase where everything had happened. It was just a set of steps. Wood, runner, spindles. It would be hoovered tomorrow. Someone would dab at the carpet with soda water, someone else would shake their head and say it would never come out. The hall would smell of baking soda for a week. Life, indecently, would go on.

But between the top step and the bottom, an entire life had fallen away. One, two, three—*Jo*—four, five, six—*no*—seven... She walked, struggled to breathe, struggled to think.

She gripped the banister until her fingers hurt and let the hurt be proof that she could still feel something.

28

December 13th

The hospital smelled of antiseptic and despair. The corridors hummed under fluorescent lights, the kind of hum that seeps into the bones, relentless and inescapable. Lucy sat hunched on a hard plastic chair, one of Ed's old hoodies clutched tightly around her body, her cheek still throbbing beneath the nurse's gauze. They had bandaged her up as soon as she arrived and told her not to go anywhere in a slightly embarrassed tone.

Every nerve in her body still rang with the sound of Josephine tumbling down the stairs, the thuds replaying in sickening rhythm.

Her mind kept stuttering, replaying the moment of self-defence, the awful give of Josephine's body, the scream cut short. She tried to remind herself she hadn't meant for it to end this way, and that she had been fighting for her life, but the memory of Josephine's eyes widening in shock was seared into her.

The sterile corridor seemed to stretch forever. Her chair wobbled slightly on the uneven vinyl floor. Opposite her, a vending machine hummed, its glass front reflecting her pale, bloodied face in distorted fragments. She hardly recognised herself.

All I do is look at my reflection, she thought, her emotions seeming a million miles away. *I look at myself and I don't recognise what I see.*

Doctors' voices drifted down the corridor from behind the double doors: clipped, efficient, stripped of emotion.

"Severe head trauma. Possible swelling on the brain. She's stable, but unresponsive."

Lucy wasn't even sure if she could really hear them. Or perhaps she was as mad as they'd tried to claim after all.

Each phrase landed like a stone. Her arms wrapped tighter around herself, trying to stop the violent tremors that seized her body. The blood had dried in the grooves of her hands, crusted in dark crescents beneath her nails. She couldn't bring herself to wash it off. To do so felt like erasing evidence, the only proof she'd been fighting for her life, not trying to take one.

The corridor door pushed open, and Susan arrived. She looked as immovable as marble, her camel coat belted with military precision, her hair smoothed into its usual severe bun. Her expression was carved from years of self-discipline and disdain.

Her heels clicked on the floor as she approached, each step echoing like a gavel in a courtroom. Lucy's throat tightened.

Susan stopped in front of her. Her eyes, cool and assessing, raked over her daughter-in-law as though she were a stain to be scrubbed out.

"Whatever happens," Susan said quietly, her voice sharper than the fluorescent light overhead, "we will always stand by our Josie."

Lucy's breath snagged. She opened her mouth to respond, but nothing came out. Her throat constricted, burning with everything she wanted to scream – that Josephine was a monster, that she had been fighting for her life, that Ed had seen. But Susan's words told her the truth: no one here would ever stand by her.

Susan didn't linger. She turned and walked down the corridor without another glance, her back as rigid as a blade.

Through the narrow window in Josephine's door, Lucy could see Ed sitting at her bedside. His head was bent low; his hand wrapped tenderly around Josephine's limp one. His thumb stroked her knuckles in the same soothing rhythm he had once used with Lucy during sleepless nights.

Henry stood behind him, his face ashen. His eyes locked on his daughter, hollow with worry, while his lips pressed into a hard line. He looked straight through Lucy as if she didn't exist, as though the woman outside the door was a stranger trespassing in their world.

That's all I've ever been to them, Lucy thought with the hard clarity of fact.

She had fought, screamed, clawed for truth and in the end, the Keaton's had closed ranks around their own. She was already a ghost to them.

~

Night deepened, swallowing the hospital into its quiet rhythms. Machines beeped steadily, nurses padded in soft-soled shoes.

Lucy remained in the corridor until her body ached from sitting. Every time she closed her eyes she saw Josephine's body tumbling, the limp heap at the bottom of the stairs. She saw Ed's face, contorted in grief, calling his sister's name.

Finally, she wandered into the main waiting room. The vending machines hummed like insects, the strip lights buzzing faintly. The chairs were lined in rows like pews in a church abandoned by God.

She lowered herself into a seat by the window. The car park below was slick with rain, lights throwing long, distorted reflections across the asphalt. She stared at her hands, still faintly stained with Josephine's blood, and finally accepted what her gut had been whispering all night.

Not all night. Weeks, Lucy. You've known this ever since she arrived.

Her marriage was over.

Ed had chosen. Whether it was guilt, history, or blood that bound him to Josephine, it no longer mattered. Lucy was the outsider, the interloper in their world. The Keaton's had slammed the door shut, and she was left out in the cold.

But she had survived.

The thought flickered weakly in her chest, half-pride, half-defiance. Josephine hadn't succeeded in killing her.

The automatic doors slid open. The sound of leather soles and the clink of metal filled the quiet. Two uniformed officers entered, their expressions grave, unreadable.

"Mrs. Keaton?" one of them said, his voice firm but not unkind.

Lucy blinked, her stomach dropping. "Yes?"

"You're under arrest for the attempted murder of your sister-in-law, Josephine Keaton."

The words struck harder than any physical blow.

"No. No, that's not," She pushed back against the chair, shaking her head. "You don't understand. She attacked me. She—"

"Please stand, ma'am." The officer's hand closed around her arm, steady but unyielding.

Lucy's breath hitched. "No! Please, listen to me! She did this. She's been tormenting me for weeks. She tried to kill me, Ed saw it all!"

Cold metal kissed her wrists as the handcuffs closed. The

sound was final, brutal. The cuffs bit into her skin, making her gasp.

They hauled her to her feet, dragging her toward the corridor. Her old trainers, the ones she threw on when running errands, squeaked against the linoleum. The sound punched her thoughts and made her want to scream.

"Please!" she cried. "You have to believe me! She set me up!"

As they passed Josephine's room, Lucy's eyes scanned the scene inside.

Josephine lay pale and motionless in the bed, tubes snaking from her arms, her face ghostly against the pillow. Ed sat rigid in the chair, his hand still clasped around hers.

Susan stood proudly at his side, her arms folded, lips pressed tight. Henry hovered just behind them; his expression locked in grief.

All three of them looked up as Lucy was dragged past, their eyes cold, unblinking.

None of them moved. None of them spoke.

Ed's gaze met hers only for a moment. His eyes were hollow, unreachable, carved by a guilt and loyalty she could never compete with. He did nothing.

Lucy stumbled, the officers pulling her upright. She could barely breathe past the panic clawing up her throat.

As she was hauled down the corridor, her sobs echoing against the sterile walls, a single truth lodged itself deep in her chest.

She had been thrown to the wolves.

She was completely alone.

And as the automatic doors opened, spilling her into the night with the rain still dripping from the roof, Lucy understood the cruellest truth of all.

Josephine had got exactly what she wanted.

Meanwhile, the rhythmic blip of the heart monitor filled the hospital room, steady but fragile, like a metronome keeping time with the storm's retreat outside. The sterile air carried a faint tang of antiseptic and latex.

Josephine lay pale against the pillows. Bandages swathed her head, and a thin line of blood had dried along her temple where it had seeped through. The rise and fall of her chest was shallow, but it was there. Alive.

Ed sat in the far corner, half in shadow. He wore his suit jacket, his shirt having been taken by the police for evidence. His face was grey, lined in ways that made him look older than his years. He sat hunched forward, elbows on his knees, staring at the space between his shoes.

He hadn't spoken since Lucy had been dragged away in handcuffs.

His silence was a riddle, an accusation, and a question all at once. Did Josephine's words replay in his head now, striking him dumb with horror? Did he have the secret knowledge that the child had been his – that they were more twisted than he could ever let anybody know? Did he know something Lucy hadn't? Or had Josephine lied and Ed had been too loyal, too blind, too shocked to say something?

He didn't look at his sister. He didn't look at his parents. He just sat there, colourless, as if the truth, whichever version of it he held, had hollowed him out.

Susan leaned over the bed, her presence softened. Her hand hovered, then descended slowly, fingers brushing Josephine's cheek. Her touch was tender, lingering, maternal, the kind of gentleness Lucy would never receive from this woman.

"There, my darling," Susan murmured, her voice a quiet murmur not meant for outsiders. "It's all over now. You're safe."

Her thumb traced a line along Josephine's jaw, smoothing the strand of hair stuck to her skin. Josephine didn't stir, didn't open her eyes, but the room seemed to lean closer, listening. Like all rooms did with Josephine. Like the whole world did.

Susan bent nearer still, her lips almost touching her daughter's ear. "Lucy will be locked away for a very long time," she whispered. "She can't hurt you now. She can't touch us. Our family can start to rebuild itself."

Henry stood at the foot of the bed; hands folded neatly in front of him. His eyes flicked from his wife to his daughter, his face unreadable, his silence complicit.

Susan's hand lingered, stroking her daughter's face with infinite patience. In that moment, she seemed to shed her steel armour, revealing the heart of a mother, a woman whose softness was only for her own.

Ed shifted slightly in his chair. His jaw tightened, his eyes flickered once toward Josephine, then away again. His silence was louder than the machines, louder than his mother's whispers. Did he believe the child had ever existed? Did he know? Or was he still caught in the undertow of Josephine's lies, too shocked to climb free?

No one asked him.

The family stayed there, the bedside tableau unbroken: Susan bending tenderly over her daughter, Henry standing stiff and watchful, Ed slumped grey and silent in the corner.

Lucy's absence weighed on the room like an open window in winter. Everything felt colder, harsher, and remained unspoken.

And at the centre of it all, Josephine lay still, her lips parted slightly, her chest rising and falling with each faint beep of the machine, the faintest curve at the corner of her mouth almost visible.

EPILOGUE

December 24th

The house is mine now.

I move through it in silence, my bare feet whispering over polished wood, and it no longer resists me the way it once did. Every corner of it has bent to me at last. A week has passed since they discharged me from the hospital: bruised, bandaged, fragile looking in the way people instinctively pity. I knew how to make the world believe I was too delicate to harm anyone, too weak to do anything but survive. And so, everyone forgave me.

Lucy didn't stand a chance.

I keep seeing her face when they dragged her away in handcuffs, white with terror, streaked with tears, her voice hoarse from screaming that she was innocent. I was unconscious, but dear Mummy told me everything down the finest details. She looked at Eddy, begging him, reaching for him with her eyes. And he didn't move. Not then. Not after. She realised in that moment what I had known all along: she had always been alone.

The neighbours talk about her now with pursed lips and low

voices, muttering about "that poor unstable woman" and "what Edward's had to endure." The police have done their part. The charges will hold. Whether Lucy ever sees the inside of a prison or not hardly matters. Her name, her reputation, her marriage are already ruined. She'll never set foot in this house again.

I no longer have to wage my war: the brakes, the dresses, the perfume, the diary, the muttering and raving in the garden in a voice pitched to perfect Lucyness. If I'm being honest, I miss it.

Her things are gone. I bagged them up myself. Her dresses, her shoes, her books with their neat little folded corners – vanished. The photographs that used to clutter the mantelpiece have been erased, one by one. The mug she always used in the mornings, the scent of her perfume on the curtains, the little traces of her presence... all scrubbed away.

It is astonishing how little of a person remains once you strip away their belongings.

The house is dressed for Christmas now. The tree glitters obediently in the corner, the smell of pine needles mingling with the faint sweetness of cinnamon. Candles flicker in the windows, their flames mirrored in the polished glass. Everything looks warm, inviting, perfect. To me it feels orderly, controlled. My order. My control.

Eddy doesn't notice. He doesn't notice anything anymore. He wanders the rooms like a ghost, silent and grey. He spends long hours upstairs in his study, the door closed, the creak of his chair the only sign he is still alive. He doesn't speak much, and when he does it is only in short, hollow phrases.

He is a prisoner here, though he doesn't yet understand it. His grief and guilt have shackled him tighter than chains ever could. He cannot leave me. He will not. In time, he'll realise there is nothing for him beyond these walls. No wife, no family but me. And when he does, he'll come to me fully.

I go into nursery which isn't a nursery anymore. Eddy

doesn't say much, but he's had one act of defiance: dismantling this sacred room. The cot, the mobile, the doll wrapped in Eddy's old shirt. All gone.

It had been almost perfect. And it will be again.

I open the wardrobe and pull out the box I hid at the back. Inside, the baby things are neatly folded: muslins, tiny socks, a cute, preloved rattle worn smooth with time. I run my fingers across them, tenderly, reverently. These objects are my promise, my inheritance. The nursery will be real one day.

People think masks are hard to wear. They aren't. They are easy, if you understand what people want from you. A victim's eyes. A tremor in the voice. A wound displayed just long enough to make others feel ashamed of doubting you. Lucy never understood that. She flailed and shouted, made scenes. She told the truth too loudly. People don't like the truth when it scratches at their comfort. They prefer the lie that lets them sleep.

So, I gave them the lie.

Now Lucy is gone, Eddy is mine to mould, and I have secured my place.

The house breathes with me now. My footsteps echo in its bones. The neighbours smile when they see me on the doorstep. My parents have closed ranks, their loyalty iron clad. The police call me "Miss Keaton" with gentleness in their tone.

I am safe.

And soon, when my perfect, handsome, deluded brother has nowhere left to go but me, when the past has softened in his mind and grief has numbed him, the nursery will be made up again, once and for all.

This time, it will not be a fantasy.

This time, it will be forever.

Printed in Dunstable, United Kingdom

72696755R00136